Reap What She Sows

A Tessa Randolph Cozy Mystery, Volume 3

Christine Zane Thomas and Paula Lester

Published by Paula Lester and Christine Zane Thomas, 2020.

Copyright Notice

This is a work of fiction. Similarities to real people, places, or events are entirely coincidental.

REAP WHAT SHE SOWS

First edition. October 30, 2020.

Copyright © 2020 Paula Lester and Christine Zane Thomas.

Written by Paula Lester and Christine Zane Thomas.

Cover Design by Mariah Sinclair at thecovervault.com

Chapter 1

"If you and I are going to give this a real shot," Silas pulled in a deep breath and then said, in a rush of words, "you're going to need to be honest about what you do. Tell me about your job—about the souls you reap."

Tessa blinked. In the week they'd spent together in Florida, Silas, her handsome landlord, had turned from friend to something else. Something more. Silas was kind and thoughtful. He was everything her previous boyfriend, Frank, wasn't. And she felt completely sideswiped by his words.

Of course, it wasn't possible for all of the air to be sucked out of the space around her, but that was how it felt for a moment. Her ears were ringing. She went cold.

She opened her mouth and then shut it again a couple of times before clamping her lips tightly together to avoid looking like a dying fish—because that was not an attractive look.

She had to admit that she *did* want to look attractive to the man in front of her. Tessa wanted him to feel how she felt. And she thought he did. Despite the fact he had just effectively outed her super-secret job as a grim reaper.

Slowly, her brain came out of its shock, and Tessa realized she had let too much time go by without answering.

How did he figure it out anyway?

Tessa knew she'd been giving off clues left and right while they were in Miami. This was all her fault. She should never have suggested that Silas use the money their neighbor, sweet Mrs. Cross, had gifted him to go on a vacation in the same place as her grim reaper convention. She'd been asking for trouble.

And there had been plenty of trouble in Florida. A reaper died on the plane and another while snorkeling. Not to mention, when out on a date with Silas, Tessa had been called to perform her duties. Silas had followed her on the job. Luckily, she hadn't actually reaped a soul then. Still, Silas had still been suspicious of what was going on.

And that hadn't been the only time he had shown skepticism about Tessa's cover story—that she was a life insurance agent. During her first week on the job, Chet Sanborn, who was a resident of their apartment building, was murdered. Unfortunately, Tessa had been late to that job and lost his soul. It'd been a mad dash to find and cross him over. Silas had been around the periphery of that crazy situation.

Okay, Tessa. It's been too long. Say something!

She went over her options. She could tell him the truth. But if she did, it could be dangerous for both of them.

Or she could lie. But lying seemed like a horrible way to start their five-second-old relationship.

She gazed into Silas' hazel eyes. They were too perfect and intent, waiting for her answer. She looked away from his eyes, studying his square jawline etched with stubble. It was no help either.

"Um." *Oh, fantastic. Just brilliant. Now he's going to think I'm unattractive and dumb.*

Good thing she was watching his jaw because then Silas broke into an adorable grin, showing the dimple in his right cheek, and he winked. "I mean, hanging out with those co-workers of yours was pretty depressing. It felt more like hanging out with a bunch of grim reapers than life insurance agents. You ever think about that?"

"About what?"

"It seems like it has the wrong name." He chuckled. "But I guess death insurance doesn't have the same ring to it."

Tessa barked out an over-the-top laugh, fueled by the relief that she felt. He'd been joking. She quickly reined it in with a gulp.

"Yeah," she squeaked. "It's hard enough to sell already. It would probably be even harder to get people to buy it with a name like that."

"Your co-workers sure have a morbid sense of humor."

She nodded. "I'm still getting used to that myself. I guess it's just one of those professions where dark humor can help you get through the hard parts."

"I can see that." Silas continued to smile.

A rush of nervous energy hit Tessa in the chest as he reached out and grabbed her hand. She sighed into his touch, lacing her fingers with his. It amazed her how new relationships always felt similar. This was the same sort of excitement she'd felt in middle school when she'd held hands with Trevor Adams on the bus.

"Well, don't you two look like peas in a pod?"

They both turned toward the voice. Tessa couldn't decide if she was relieved or annoyed at the interruption.

Old Mrs. Cross hobbled toward the building. She wasn't exactly Tessa's favorite person—she'd told everyone who would listen that Tessa probably killed Chet Sanborn. But Tessa had been raised to be respectful of elders, and the woman *had* given Silas a lovely gift of money when she won some from a scratch-off ticket.

Mrs. Cross stopped in front of them, leaned on her flower-patterned cane, and peered, first at Tessa, then at Silas, and then down to their interlocked hands. The old woman was hunched at the shoulders. She craned her neck to see their faces. Tessa wondered how much taller the woman had been in her youth, before age had weighed her down.

"Are you two an item now?" she croaked.

Tessa thought there was a hint of jealousy in her tone. She felt a squirm gathering in her spine and tried to fight it off, not wanting to act like a naughty schoolgirl in front of the woman. She let go of Silas's hand and shifted her eyes away from Mrs. Cross's stone gaze. She found her shoes instead, a pair of red Chuck Taylors.

Next to her, Silas's voice was smooth and light. "Well, I don't know if item is the right word, but Tessa and I are dating." He put an arm around her shoulders and drew her in closer to his side.

Tessa blew out the breath she'd been holding and relaxed. Lifting her chin, she met Mrs. Cross's gaze again, more confident this time.

"Well, I suppose that's just fine, then," Mrs. Cross said with a nod. "Both of you are good-looking and about the same age. Same socioeconomic status too, I'll wager." She nodded again and then moved forward, forcing Tessa and Silas to leap apart or have their feet tromped on by her cane as she elbowed between them.

For the second time in a ten-minute span, Tessa found her jaw dropped open. Mrs. Cross certainly wasn't up on political correctness, with her talk about them being attractive and all that. She glanced at Silas, who grinned back at her and gave her a wink. Tessa had been right—there was definitely some jealousy there.

"Silas, dear," Mrs. Cross grabbed his elbow to steady herself, "my showerhead is dripping. You'll need to come by and fix it this afternoon while I'm at my hair appointment. I don't want to have to listen to your tools making a big noise in that echoey bathroom."

She let go of his arm, and Silas rushed forward to open the door for Mrs. Cross just as she arrived at it. "You bet, Mrs. Cross. I'll take care of that showerhead while you're at your appointment. It'll be good as new when you get back."

The elderly woman reached up and patted his cheek. "Such a good boy," she said as she disappeared into Mist River Manor's lobby.

Silas turned back toward Tessa. "She sure is a pistol, isn't she?"

"That's one word for it, I guess."

He shrugged. "Yeah. She's rough around the edges, that's for sure. I just try to keep her happy. At her age, she deserves that."

Tessa crossed her arms and gave him a mischievous look. "I really don't think that meeting the unreasonable demands of old ladies is part of your job description."

"It's not *just* the old ladies I try to keep happy. I want everybody to enjoy living here."

"I seem to remember you giving me a hard time when I couldn't make rent on time every month," she teased.

He widened his eyes to look innocent. "I don't own this place. I'm just the landlord. When it comes to the accounting, my hands are tied. Besides, I always tried to give you a few extra days whenever I could." He tipped his head. "But you seem to be making enough at this new job that it isn't an issue anymore."

Oops. Too late, Tessa realized her mistake. The conversation had steered away from her job as a grim reaper, and here she'd brought it right back around to the same spot she'd been trying to avoid.

"Hey, do you want to have dinner tonight?"

Shew! He hadn't taken the opportunity to question her more about her job. This time. Tessa knew it would come up again, though. She was going to have to practice not imitating a tongue-tied fish every time he did if she wanted this relationship to work.

"Dinner sounds great! You should come to my place." *Wait. What?* Why in the world had she said that?

"Oh, wow. I'd love a chance to try your cooking. How about I come by around six?"

"Six is perfect!" She smiled through a wince. *Aargh.* It was as though her mouth was not attached to her brain at all. Why did that happen to her so often? She should really talk to a doctor about it.

"Okay. Well, I'll see you then."

With a heart-stoppingly gorgeous smile, Silas leaned in and kissed Tessa's cheek before allowing her to step through the open door.

Her heart started pounding again as she crossed the lobby. Why had she invited Silas to her place? That was the worst possible idea. The most obvious reason for that being she was a terrible cook. Her mind raced through the dishes she knew how to make, and she grimaced.

She couldn't make him ramen—they weren't broke college students. Mac and cheese was out too because it didn't always turn out great for Tessa. More often than not, it was either too mushy or overly crunchy.

Okay, okay. Calm down, Tessa. You can figure this out. Google is your friend.

She knew Silas liked empanadas. Maybe she could find an easy recipe for that.

Tessa felt a little better. Until she opened the door to her apartment.

She groaned and slumped into the door frame.

The place was an absolute wreck. Like, hurricane-level messy. Every piece of clothing she owned was strewn across the floor and furniture. Dishes sat piled in the sink and spilling out onto the counter next to it. And there were clumps of cat fur dotting the living room carpet.

Cat fur. Oh, no. She was absolutely not supposed to have a cat.

As though the thought had conjured her, Pepper sauntered over and rubbed on Tessa's shins. With a little shriek, Tessa bolted the rest of the way through the doorway and shut the door tightly behind her.

She couldn't have Silas come over. He'd see Pepper. Even though they were dating, he'd feel bound to tell her to get rid of the pet because those were the rules. And she couldn't ask him to risk his job for her sassy ball of fur.

She let her head clunk back against the door. "What am I going to do?"

Pepper purred loudly and headed for the kitchen, apparently thinking the answer to Tessa's rhetorical question was that it was cat food time.

"Cuz you *always* think with your stomach, you brat." But Tessa obediently followed Pepper and dumped some kibble into her bowl. "There."

The tortie sat and looked up at her, grumpiness written all over her face.

"No. I'm not giving you canned food. You're getting chunky. You can have some canned food tomorrow morning." Tessa crossed her arms and tried to sound firm.

Pepper yowled and then stalked away, leaving the kibble untouched.

Tessa narrowed her eyes at the cat's retreating tail. Maybe her friend, Abi, would take the cat for the evening, so Silas wouldn't see her.

But she shook her head to dismiss the idea. If she and Silas were going to be dating, he would be at her apartment sometimes. She couldn't hide the food, litter, and fur. And she couldn't deposit Pepper at Abi's every time. Abi absolutely hated the cat after babysitting her while Tessa was in Florida.

No, if the cat was going to cause an issue between them, it was probably better to get it over with right away.

With that decided, Tessa puffed a piece of dark hair out of her eyes, rolled up her sleeves, and attacked the dirty dishes.

Letting him see the cat was one thing. She didn't need to reveal her slobby side to the man quite yet. Because, as much as she tried to tell herself the place was messy because she'd lost control of it between packing for Florida, being gone, and jumping right back into work when she got home, the truth was her apartment was always a wreck.

As she scrubbed dirty dishes, Tessa's mind wandered, and she felt a twinge of discomfort.

Was it fair to Silas to begin a relationship with him when he didn't know the whole truth about her life? And she really didn't intend to tell him anytime soon.

After all, having a cat, being a bit of a slob, and not having any sort of cooking skills whatsoever was just the tip of her secret-berg.

Chapter 2

It turned out that, according to the internet, empanadas were way too complicated. That wasn't exactly true. The internet tried to make everything sound simple. But Tessa could read through the lines of every recipe and video she found. She wasn't going to be able to make them. Not now, probably not ever.

She spent a frantic ten minutes pulling all the ingredients she could find out of her cupboards onto the counter. Then she rummaged through the refrigerator and freezer, finally deciding her best bet was spaghetti. That shouldn't be too hard to mess up—it only required that she boil some noodles, brown some meat, and add some sauce.

Plus, in the back of the freezer, she'd found a forgotten loaf of garlic bread that made her fist pump the air in victory. Maybe this would be a good dinner after all.

Once the sauce with meat was simmering and she'd added the noodles to boiling water, Tessa made a pass through the house, gathering every bit of clothing she came upon into her arms. She tossed the whole pile into the closet in her bedroom, giving it a kick to get it all inside. The door didn't want to close, but she managed to heave it shut with a grunt of satisfaction.

The apartment looked much better when she walked back through. And there was no way Silas would ever go into her bedroom and peek in the closet. Not only would he think she was a good cook, but, hopefully, he'd also believe she was a neat and tidy person.

She pulled the vacuum out of the closet in the hallway and had to spend a little time fiddling with the unfamiliar controls to get it the right height for the area rug in the living room, which confirmed what she already knew in her heart—she didn't vacuum up Pepper's fur balls nearly often enough.

It was getting close to six. She lit a vanilla-scented candle in the living room, crossed her arms, and looked around. She was going to pull this off. She pushed back her shoulders, feeling a bit smug.

Then the smoke alarm went off in the kitchen.

With a squeal, Tessa raced into the room. Smoke billowed out of the noodle pan. Luckily, she had the foresight to grab a hot mitt before pulling the pan off the heat. She waited for the big billow of smoke to dissipate before she carefully peeked in, against a wave of trepidation.

Tessa groaned. The pot had run dry, and what had once been noodles was now a pile of unrecognizable, charred material stuck to the bottom of the pan.

After she'd redone the noodles—luckily she had another box, and this time she stood right in front of the stove and watched it like a hawk—Tessa had to rush to get herself changed and ready, barely finishing applying her mascara before she heard a knock at the door.

For as much as her nerves were jittering over the state of her apartment and whether dinner would be edible, Tessa felt a thrill of anticipation about having another date with Silas. They'd had such a good time going out in the evenings after her work conference presentations in Florida. But, somehow, having him over to her apartment for a nice, intimate dinner felt much more as though they were dating and less like they were just meeting up as friends.

As she hurried out of the bedroom, Tessa found Pepper sitting just inside the doorway with her head tilted.

"I know that look," Tessa hissed. "You stay out of sight and don't make trouble. If you do that—if and only if you do that—I'll give you half a can of cat food after Silas leaves."

For good measure, Tessa closed the bedroom door with the cat inside. Maybe Silas wouldn't notice the food bowls and Tessa could continue to get away with having a pet in the apartment, even though she wasn't supposed to.

She didn't have to fake the smile on her face when she opened the door. Tessa was genuinely glad to welcome Silas in. "You look handsome."

He waved his hands up and down his own body with a flick of the wrists. "This old thing?" He shrugged. "It's basically my only nice outfit, so it doesn't get worn too often."

"Jeans and a plaid flannel shirt are your only nice outfit?" Tessa stepped to the side so Silas could enter.

"I live in Michigan—what do you expect my nice clothes to look like?"

Tessa chuckled. "I suppose plaid and denim are just fine. This place is a little bit messy. Sorry about that."

She wasn't kidding either. She'd missed a few things. There were still magazines strewn across the coffee table, a few dirty dishes she hadn't gotten to piled on the kitchen counter, and a layer of dust covering the TV shelf in the living room. But that was fine with her. After all, she really didn't want to offer up a complete facade of what her life was like.

But he didn't need to know that a half-hour earlier, virtually every piece of clothing she owned had littered the place from one end to the other.

"Looks good to me," he said, "and smells even better." He sniffed the air, reminding her of a bloodhound. "Is that spaghetti and . . . vanilla?"

Tessa grinned and waved a hand. "The vanilla isn't edible. It's just a candle. I *did* make spaghetti and—oh no!" She darted for the kitchen, remembering she'd shoved the garlic bread into the oven before she went to put on her makeup.

She grabbed hot mitts and opened the oven door, expecting to again see black smoke billowing in her kitchen. She was pleasantly surprised. Golden brown bread, bubbling away, greeted her with the heavenly smell of garlic and butter. With a sigh of relief, she pulled out the pan and set it on the empty stove burners.

"That looks great." Silas leaned on the doorjamb. "I love Italian."

"Well, unless you love Americanized Italian, you're out of luck. Because we're dining on Italian-American, mostly out of a jar, tonight."

He dipped his head, dimples popping in his cheeks. "American-Italian out of a jar is my favorite kind of Italian. I mean, really, is there another way?"

She smirked, thinking of her mother. Cheryl cooked everything from scratch and was a master chef in the kitchen. Those genes hadn't passed down to her. She'd gotten her father's cooking skills. Alone one weekend, with her mother gone to a conference—which Tessa now realized was the reaper conference like she'd just attended—her father had burnt a record number of grilled cheese sandwiches before giving up and ordering pizza.

"Do you need a hand with anything?" Silas asked.

"Yeah, grab a plate out of there." She gestured at a cupboard over her head. "And here's a towel. You can make sure the bread stays warm while I drain the noodles."

As soon as the words were out of Tessa's mouth, she realized she'd made a horrible mistake. She'd taken the noodles off the heat but left them in the hot water while she went to change her clothes.

With a wince, she peered into the pot. They looked all right. Maybe everything would be fine. At the very least, they weren't a pile of stinky ash like the pot she'd shoved under the sink in hopes the stench wouldn't escape.

When she got to the tiny dining room table just outside the kitchen with the drained noodles and sauce, she found that Silas had not only taken care of the garlic bread, but he'd also found plates, silverware, and cups and set two places.

"Oh! That reminds me." She set down the food, turned on her heel, and went back into the kitchen to retrieve the bottle of Merlot she'd opened and left to breathe a while earlier. For half a second, she felt proud for orchestrating a lovely meal.

The pride only lasted a few more minutes because when Tessa bit into her pasta, it was mushy and all stuck together. "Oh, no. I overcooked the noodles."

But Silas was munching away. Around a bite, he said, "I think it's awesome. It tastes just like my mom's spaghetti. With us kids always around, she must've overdone the noodles too. Normally, I don't like anybody else's spaghetti. I guess most people cook the noodles al dente. Not my style."

She pursed her lips and studied his face. Was he for real or just trying to make her feel better?

With a tiny shrug, Tessa decided she didn't care. She chose to believe Silas liked the meal, and she dug in, determined to enjoy it too, even though it was a bit—well, actually a lot—on the mushy side.

As they both finished their spaghetti, Tessa suddenly realized something. "I'm so sorry. I don't have anything for dessert."

Silas pushed his plate aside and pulled the wine goblet in front of him. "This is good enough for me. I'm stuffed. Thank you for dinner." Suddenly, he leaned forward and locked eyes with her. "But you really have to do something about the cat. You know you're not allowed to have one."

Her eyes fluttered for a second. How did he know about Pepper?

Then, she sighed as she caught sight of the tortie's tail peeking out from under the table. Tessa leaned sideways to see that the cat was weaving her way in a figure-eight around Silas's feet. "How did you get out?" she demanded.

"Out? Did she lock you in somewhere?" Silas sounded shocked, and he leaned down to scratch Pepper's forehead.

"Um. Well, I just thought it would be nice to eat without her fur flying into our food. We're lucky she's not on the table."

"Really? So, you didn't lock her away so I wouldn't happen to see her?" A muscle jumped in his lip, and Tessa realized he was holding back a smile.

She blew out a breath. "Okay, I'm sorry. And, by the way, I think she may be more than a cat. Like, I suspect the little brat may be part witch or something because I have no idea how she managed to open a closed bedroom door and get out here. Seriously, though, you have to let me keep her. I don't have anyone to give her to."

"What about your mom? Didn't you tell me she lives alone? Maybe she could use some company."

"My mom?" Tessa leaned back and barked out a laugh. "No, my mom does not need a cat. I mean, yes, she lives alone, but no, she doesn't need a companion. She doesn't get along with roommates very well. Other than my dad, that is, and he . . . he passed away."

"Maybe she's lonely. You can't assume she wouldn't want a roommate, can you?"

"Oh, I think I can. My mom likes things just so. I couldn't get out of her house fast enough when I went to college, and I never went back home. Mom's never had any kind of a pet or roommate or anything else like that since I left. If it was something she wanted, she could've gotten it for herself a long time ago."

He held up his hands, palms out. "Okay, okay. I'll pretend like I didn't see her here tonight. But you have to keep her away from the windows."

Tessa pulled the cat, who had left Silas and come to rub on her shins, into her lap. "I will." She rubbed her face on Pepper's. "You'll stay away from the windows, won't you, girl?"

"Does she understand English?"

"She understands it well enough to do the exact opposite of everything I ask her to do," Tessa said. She tossed the cat gently onto the floor. "So, what do you have planned for tomorrow?"

"I have a ton to do to get this place ready for winter. There's some caulking, some nailing, some siding replacement, some painting, and lots of getting the pool ready to winterize. You know, all the fun stuff. How about you?"

She shrugged. "Same old, same old. Just another day at work."

"Riiiight. Work."

"Work," she repeated. "Selling life insurance."

"You're still sticking to that story, huh?"

The flash of irritation in her gut surprised Tessa. But she couldn't push it down. How many times were they going to have to revisit this topic? She'd thought the conversation they'd had earlier would be the end of it, at least for a while.

But here he was, trying to poke holes in her story again.

Without taking a moment to think better of it, she snapped, "Can we give that a rest, please?"

Silas' jaw dropped a fraction before he snapped it shut. "I'm sorry. It's just that I can't shake the feeling that something isn't quite right about that job of yours. It just . . . feels like there's something more to it than selling life insurance." He twirled the wine glass between his fingers. "I keep thinking about that girl on the pier. The one who almost fell in."

"Dani." The name came out before Tessa could stop it.

A line appeared on Silas's forehead. "Yeah. Dani. Funny that you remember her name. That whole thing seemed so strange. I swear it was like you knew it was going to happen ahead of time and rushed straight to that spot to save her." He leaned forward and spoke in a low voice, as though Pepper may overhear and spread gossip about it. "Are you . . . are you, like, a superhero or something?"

The bit of irritation had flared into something brighter as Silas spoke. "No, I'm not. I'm just a life insurance agent."

"Right. Just a life insurance agent. But for real, if you *are* a superhero, I'm happy to be your Mary Jane. Or Lois Lane—I'd make a great reporter. You know, there really isn't a guy version of those two. What a crock."

"Silas, I'm not a hero."

"Something *is* up though. I can see you want to tell me. You should just do it."

"Nothing is up! If you can't accept what I tell you, then maybe this whole thing is a bad idea."

She regretted the words as soon as they left her mouth.

But it was too late. Silas's jaw clenched. He pushed back from the table. "You know, I think I'm going to head home. Long day tomorrow. Do you need help with dishes or anything?"

A lump formed in her throat. She wanted to apologize for being so mean. But the words wouldn't come. She just shook her head.

"Okay. Well, thanks again for dinner. It really was just like my mom's. I'll see you later, Tessa."

And, just like that, he was gone, and Tessa was staring at the closed door, hating the sudden silence.

She felt terrible.

Chapter 3

It took Tessa's brain a few minutes to properly identify the input and process it as something happening to her physical body rather than a dream occurrence. When it did, the awful dream she was having ended. It was something to do with sandpaper—her mother using it to scrub off paint on Tessa's elbow. Only now, with the dream over, there was still something rough and moist lashing over and over her skin like an old cassette tape on repeat.

Tessa bolted upright in bed. Pepper sat beside her, looking innocent.

Tessa rubbed her arm and scolded. "Really? Licking me with that horrible tongue without my consent? I was fast asleep. That's pretty rude."

The cat didn't act contrite in the slightest. She reached out and gave Tessa's arm another swipe with her barbed tongue.

Tessa jerked her arm away and shrieked, "Stop that! You're not getting any canned food anyway. We had a deal. You didn't stay away from Silas last night."

As soon as the words were out of her mouth, Tessa groaned and put her face in her hands.

Silas. Had they really fought last night? Is that what that had been?

But that wasn't the only reason she held her head in her hands. It felt heavy, and she was having trouble remembering the details about last night with Silas because she'd finished the bottle of wine alone after he left.

A full cup of water sat untouched on the nightstand. A good thought, had she drunk any of it.

She sipped and made herself think about the previous evening for a few minutes. She and Silas hadn't really had a back-and-forth type of argument, but she hadn't been very nice to him when he asked about her job. He'd left pretty abruptly.

Yep. That had definitely been a fight.

Tessa felt horrible, and not just from the hangover. She shouldn't have reacted the way she did to Silas' questions. The only reason she had was because she felt so insecure about that entire subject. Should she come clean and tell him that she was a reaper? Or keep grasping for a lie that he would accept?

It felt terrible to lie when they were just embarking on a new relationship but telling him made her feel uneasy too. To an outsider, her job would be pretty unbelievable. Chances were, he wouldn't even believe her.

But she was going to have to make a decision about how to handle this issue and then stick to it. Waffling, even in her own mind, wasn't working out at all.

Tessa hauled herself out of bed and grabbed the phone to check the reaper app. It'd become a habit to do that first thing in the morning, so she didn't miss any assignments. Sure enough, there was one waiting for her, and she checked the time of death against the digital clock on the end table. She had forty-five minutes.

Tessa scrolled through the assignment to see where she needed to go and frowned, not recognizing the address. Luckily, the reaper app was set up for such things, and she tapped the screen until a map pulled up. It didn't look like it would be hard to find, and it wasn't too far away. Tessa decided she had time for a quick shower, but she'd have to miss breakfast if she did that.

A grumbling rumble in her stomach made it clear that Tessa's body was more interested in breakfast than a shower. So, she only washed her face, ran a brush through her long, dark hair, and pulled on jeans and a sweater before heading toward sustenance.

Pepper did her best to trip Tessa all the way down the hallway, through the living room, and into the kitchen. "No. I said you can't have any canned food. Here's your kibble." Tessa sprinkled some dry food into the cat's bowl. Pepper gave her a look of extreme betrayal, and it made Tessa giggle. "Okay, okay. You can have a quarter of a can. How's that?"

Pepper licked her nose and appeared eager, so Tessa took that as acquiescence and dished out the cat food. Then she got a pot of coffee started, poured herself a bowl of cereal, and carried it to the dining room table.

The scene of the crime. She tried not to think about Silas while she ate but wasn't very successful. She racked her brain, trying to figure out how she could make things right with him.

And she *did* want to make things right. He was a good guy, and she had a feeling he'd make a fantastic boyfriend. They just had to get through this rough patch.

Once she'd filled a giant glittery purple travel mug with hot java and petted Pepper goodbye, Tessa left the apartment. She wasn't sure whether she wanted to run into Silas in the lobby or not. A glance at her fitness watch—which she used almost exclusively for telling time and fashion and almost never for fitness—told her she didn't have the time to run into him.

Luckily, the lobby was empty, and Tessa scooted out without having to talk to anyone.

Linda, Tessa's 1981 Buick LeSabre, fired right up. Tessa let out a breath, relieved. For a long time, Linda had been sort of finicky, but she'd been reliable enough never to leave Tessa stranded anywhere. At least since Silas had taken over her upkeep, the car had been running better than it had in years. Still, whenever Tessa was on a deadline—especially to get to a reap—she was always a bit nervous about the car's performance.

Tessa set her phone on the passenger seat with the reaper app open to the map screen. She gulped coffee as fast as possible while she drove. She was grateful when the dull pounding in her head began to recede as the caffeine hit her bloodstream.

The destination was just outside of Mist River, where the properties were large and the homes even bigger. It had always been strange to Tessa that Mist River was such a sleepy little town but that this sprawling neighborhood of mansions was so close. Cheryl said most of the people who owned them worked in the big city and either commuted daily or the family stayed in Mist River while the breadwinner only came home on the weekends.

Tessa remembered attending a few house parties in this neighborhood during high school. The extravagance had shocked her. One place had both an indoor and outdoor pool. *Two beautiful pools*! At the time, Tessa had to go to the local YMCA to use *one* pool—and that one had broken tiles with green stuff growing around the edges and questionable chlorine levels.

The assignment's address delivered Tessa to the mouth of a driveway so long that she couldn't see the house at the end of it. The driveway was paved and lined with huge maples on both sides, the branches of which leaned in toward each other, meeting in a canopy high above the ground.

Wow. In another month or so, that would make a stunning tunnel of gold, yellow, and red. It almost made her want to make a note to come back and see it when autumn leaves were at their peak.

About ten feet into the driveway stood a spectacular wrought iron gate in two pieces designed to meet and lock in the center. Only one side was open. If Tessa scooted the car a tiny bit onto the shoulder, she'd be able to squeeze the LeSabre through the opening.

That's weird. You'd think a place like this would be locked up tight all the time.

But a glance at the clock told Tessa she didn't have time to consider such things. She only had about five minutes to find Mr. Artemis Green before he died.

She gave Linda a little bit of gas to nudge her through the gate, but the car didn't respond other than to let out an ominous cough-bark-wheeze sound. Tessa pushed the gas again, a bit more insistently, but it was no use. Linda's engine sputtered to a stop. With a quick curse, Tessa twisted the key in the ignition. "Come on, come on," she muttered.

But Linda didn't even attempt to start up. There was just . . . nothing.

Tessa chewed on her bottom lip for a second, debating what to do. She looked at her watch. There wasn't much of a choice. She grabbed her phone, jumped out of the car, and ran up the driveway.

She estimated the driveway was about a quarter mile long, and by the time the house came into view, Tessa was mouth-breathing in an attempt to drag enough oxygen into her lungs to power her legs. Pain exploded in her side, and she leaned over, trying to relax the stitch while berating herself for not hitting the treadmill more often. Or at all.

Still gasping, she craned her neck to gawk at the gorgeous architectural structure in front of her.

The place was gigantic, towering at least four stories high, with grand turrets in three spots on top of it. The grounds surrounding the house were immaculate. It looked like someone had gone around trimming the grass with a pair of scissors, and the flowerbeds didn't appear to have a single weed among them. They were filled with beautifully trimmed hedges, rosebushes with flowers in every hue, and gorgeous orange, yellow, white, and brilliant purple gladiolus. Tessa recognized rhododendron bushes that were almost two stories high. Though the time for them to flower had long past, she could imagine how striking they would look in late spring.

The house's footprint would probably take up a Mist River city block, and a huge porch stretched the entire length of its front and wrapped around both sides.

Tessa only considered sprinting up the steps and knocking on the door for an instant. But her instincts and the recent reaper training in Miami told her that was foolish. She'd almost certainly run into staff members or perhaps Mr. Green's family if she tried to make a frontal assault like that.

She straightened, feeling glad the stitch in her side had eased, and sprinted around the side of the house. Movement to the left caught her eye, and she lunged behind a hedge.

Okay. Get yourself together. Remember what you learned at the conference.

At the time, the presentation about keeping to the shadows had seemed laughable. But now she had to use the information, so Tessa wracked her brain to remember what Bubba had said.

So far, she hadn't done a great job of sticking to any shadows. She'd taken in the lovely architecture but just now spotted the two cameras perched at the corners of the house. She made a note to steer clear of them and to look out for more.

For a second, she wished for the secret of invisibility that the original grim reaper had bestowed upon Lee Stuart. He hadn't deserved it, but she could sure make good use of it now. A glance around the hedge told her it was a gardener she'd seen moving about, and she was still out there, trimming fruit tree branches with a huge pinchy tool.

She really should pay more attention when her mother tried to teach her about taking care of plants.

Tessa looked around wildly, knowing without checking that she was running out of time to get to Artemis Green. She couldn't miss his death and lose his soul.

Been there. Done that. Got the T-shirt.

She crouched low and darted to the next hedge, staying close to the house and keeping an eye on the gardener. She continued that way, needles falling into her hair and branches scraping her arms, until she got around the house into the back yard.

Tessa didn't see anyone, but the expanse of the area was huge. The landscape was dotted with flower beds, small groves of trees, and even a couple bubbling fountains with seating around them. About an acre away stood a huge red barn, complete with a couple of horses in an attached paddock.

There could easily be someone tucked into one of those areas, working, and Tessa wouldn't be able to see them.

She studied the back of the house. The wraparound porch extended all the way along its length, too, and Tessa counted at least four doors on this side of the house. She wasn't sure which one to try.

With a frown, she pulled out her phone and checked the reaper app again, quickly scanning the assignment details. *The kitchen*. It was supposed to happen in the kitchen on the west side of the house.

She slipped the phone into her pocket, checked for a camera, then quickly climbed the stairs onto the porch, making her way to the westernmost doorway. She was in the open now, but it couldn't be helped. She'd need to rely on being quick to keep from being spotted if anyone *was* in the back yard to spot her.

When she got to the door, Tessa drew in a deep breath and reached out to try it. When it gave under her hand and opened, she let the breath out and popped her head through the doorway. *Yes*! It was a kitchen. A huge, gleaming, stainless steel kitchen that looked like it should be absolutely bustling with staff, creating meals for dozens of people at a time.

Only it wasn't. There was only one person visible in the kitchen, and he had his back to Tessa. He sat at the bar in a corner of the kitchen, which was made up to be a breakfast nook, surrounded by walls of windows overlooking the back gardens.

For a second, she wondered if the man with a salt-and-pepper crewcut and a green polo shirt tucked carefully into black slacks was Artemis Green, her assignment, or someone else. He almost looked too young and fit to be the seventy-five years he was supposed to be.

But when the man's spine stiffened and then quickly slumped, his head diving straight into his cereal bowl, Tessa knew she had the right person.

In a few seconds, Artemis Green's soul rose from his body. He glanced at Tessa and then back at his body, which was still.

Spirit Artemis tsked as milk flowed over the edges of the bowl and onto the bar. "What a pity. If I'd known this would be my last meal, I would've chosen the marshmallow cereal over the bran."

"Hey, I had marshmallow today!" Tessa blurted out. Then she winced, pretty sure she committed a faux pas.

But Artemis grinned. "Good for you. Of course, it's good to keep your body healthy, but we should all splurge once in a while. After all, you never know when your last day will be, even if you take excellent care of yourself."

Tessa studied the man, both the spirit and physical versions. "It looks like you were in great shape."

He nodded. "Oh, yes. I saw my doctor just last week. Had a stress test and he said the old ticker was like one a thirty-year-old man would have. I exercised at least a couple of hours a day—cardio and weight training. My cholesterol was tip-top, and I never had a lick of trouble with my blood pressure. Of course, my life wasn't without stress." A shadow passed over his expression. He shook it off and smiled. "But, in general, I was very healthy."

Tessa shook her head sadly and flicked a wrist to open a portal to the other side of the veil. As bright light spilled over them, Artemis looked at his body one last time. "I don't think that bran tasted quite right. I should know because I had it every day for fifteen years. No, as I said, I was healthy as one of the horses in the barn out back." He pinned her with eyes that still managed to look sharp, even though they were in the face of a semi-transparent spirit. "I think you'll find that I didn't die of natural causes. I'm sure I was poisoned."

Tessa was still pondering what he'd said after she released the path across the veil. But she knew it was important for her to get out of there before someone saw her. Figuring that heading back the way she'd come was her best bet for staying hidden, she turned on her heel to head out the back door but staggered to a halt after only one step, a gasp erupting from her throat.

His face the same cream color as the kitchen walls around him and his jaw hanging slack, Silas stood between Tessa and the back door.

Chapter 4

For what felt like five minutes but was probably about half a second, Tessa mirrored Silas's shocked expression. Then, she sprang forward.

"We have to get out of here," she hissed.

But Silas was craning his neck to get a better look at Mr. Green. Tessa ducked around him. She grabbed him by the elbow, spun him around, and yanked him toward the door.

But his feet were planted. He may as well have been a giant boulder for as far as she was able to move him. Like a dog hitting the end of a leash, Tessa jerked to a stop and lurched backward a bit, bungling into him. This sent her landlord's formerly inert feet the other direction—toward the deceased body.

He steadied himself on the back of Mr. Green's chair. Touching objects in and around a reap was definitely something Bubba had mentioned as a faux pas. Although Tessa had been guilty of it before. It was the new information—the notion that Mr. Green believed he'd been poisoned—that made Tessa cringe.

He let go, and she wiped his prints away with the underside of her shirt.

"We really have to go." She'd either have to keep going without him or stay there. And she knew that, like it or not, it was her fault Silas was there. She couldn't just leave him.

"What just happened?" Silas's voice was hushed but not a whisper, like Tessa would've preferred.

Her eyes darted toward the second doorway in the kitchen, the one that led to the rest of the house, and she licked her lips. "I'll explain, but we have to go."

Silas shook his head a fraction in each direction. He looked over his shoulder at Artemis's body. "He's dead, you know."

Tessa nodded. "He is."

"Is he one of your clients?"

"I guess you could say that. Silas, I'm serious. We have to go. Now!" She kept watching the doorway. If someone came through it, they would see Tessa and Silas immediately. There was no way they could blend in with the stainless steel appliances. Especially since Silas seemed to be still trying to hold on to the Florida vibes.

He was still tanned. And he was wearing a short sleeve, button-down shirt that had an orange background and was covered in yellow, blue, and salmon-colored flowers—not something most Michiganders wore when fall touched the air.

"We should probably call 9-1-1," Silas said, still unmoving.

"No. We should go. I'm trying to tell you we need to leave."

"Tessa, did you kill that man?" He jabbed a finger toward the body. Tessa reached out and snatched Silas's hand, pulling him toward the door again. "I promise you'll get all your answers. But not here. As soon as we're out of here, I'll tell you everything."

Tessa realized she wasn't lying. She would tell Silas the truth. The whole truth. In hindsight, she wished she already had.

Silas moved, then, though he still seemed reluctant. *Whatever.* Tessa would take it. As long as he was walking, she could work with that.

Her heart pounded as they rushed through the back door onto the porch and ran down its length. Tessa tried to use the skills she'd acquired in years of dance to bounce on the balls of her feet quietly as she ran. Silas seemed to take a hint from what she was doing, and she could only hear the barest of footfalls behind her.

Wow. She remembered he'd played baseball. Maybe he was incorporating his base running skills. Whatever it was, she was grateful that he was light on his feet. Hopefully, they wouldn't draw any attention.

But that was more than could be hoped for. As they neared the end of the house, Tessa glanced toward the horse barn and saw four gorgeous specimens lined up against the fence, staring at her and Silas curiously.

Well, at least the horses couldn't blab about who they'd seen.

"Come on," she whispered over her shoulder. "We need to go faster." She dropped Silas's hand and darted around the corner, keeping close to the house, behind the hedges, again.

When they got to the front of the house, there was nowhere else to remain under cover. If it was just Tessa, she may have tried to stay toward the edge of the lawn, among the landscaping there, but Silas's shirt was never going to blend in with Michigan's flora. So, she decided the best thing they could do was simply make a run for it.

She pumped her arms and legs and ran straight down the middle of the driveway. She could hear Silas just behind her, allowing her to lead the way.

They made it about halfway, and Tessa was just beginning to think maybe they'd be okay, when the mansion behind them seemed to erupt into chaos.

It began with one horrendously loud screech, and Tessa knew someone had found Artemis Green. After that, multiple shouts and screams drifted to them from behind. Tessa put on speed, ignoring the aching muscles that were screaming for more oxygen. She scooted through the still-open gate and skidded to a halt next to Linda, dragging open the door and throwing herself inside. She was gratified when Silas climbed in the passenger seat without further trying to slow her down. But when she turned the key in the ignition, Linda didn't respond at all.

"No!" she cried. "Not now." Tessa knew it had been too much to hope that the car had gotten over whatever snit she'd been in when they arrived at the mansion. She shot Silas a horrified look.

He was staring at her, not much having changed in his expression or complexion since she'd first turned around to find him in the kitchen. "I knew you were lying to me, but I never expected this."

Tessa tried firing up the car again. This time, an annoying clicking sound was Linda's only response. "I know this looks crazy bad. And I swear I'll explain it, but . . ."

He cut her off. "Did that guy want to die? Is that what kind of agency you work for? A Kevorkian thing?"

So, he hadn't seen the whole thing. Silas had obviously shown up sometime after Artemis died. She shook her head. "That isn't it. I don't do assisted suicides." Tessa tried to keep her tone calm and soft. It must have been a huge shock for Silas to see Tessa standing there next to a newly dead person.

Still, why was he there? Obviously, he'd followed her.

Again.

A siren sounded. Too close.

Tessa twisted in the seat to pin Silas with her best schoolteacher look. "Silas. We need to get out of here." She emphasized each word. "I will explain everything when we're safe. But right now, I need your help."

The very last thing she wanted to do was try to come up with an explanation for why the two of them were at Artemis Green's house when he died.

For ten excruciating seconds, Silas stared at her. She watched his jaw work, probably mimicking the gears in his mind as he thought over the situation. Then he barked, "Pop the hood," and jumped out.

Thank goodness. She did what he asked and then turned to watch the road, ready to burst out of her skin with nerves as the sirens got louder. "Okay, calm down, Tessa. It's totally fine. No one saw you in the house except the horses. All you have to do is say your car stalled on the road, and you turned in here."

Having the alibi ready calmed her some, and her heart slowed. She could hear Silas doing something under the hood and feel the car moving as he leaned against the front fender.

Without warning, the hood slammed. Silas jumped back in the passenger side. "She'll start now. Let's go."

"What about your truck?" She twisted the key and puffed out a breath when the engine came to life, even though it was more of a whimper than a roar. It didn't matter. Linda was running. She put it in reverse and stepped on the gas.

"It's down the road a bit." He gestured the right direction, and Tessa went that way. An ambulance, then three police cars passed them, squealing into Artemis's driveway.

Tessa had the ridiculous thought that they would have to hop out and open the other side of the gate for the ambulance to fit through.

Silas said, "If you don't explain to me what I just saw, my brain is going to explode."

Tessa pulled onto the shoulder behind Silas' truck. "Let's get back to my apartment, okay?"

He didn't answer. Instead, he said, "If it's not assisted suicide then, what?" He barked out a thin laugh tinged with hysteria and brushed floppy hair out of his eyes. "I know. You're the grim reaper."

When she didn't laugh at his attempt at a joke, his face stilled, eyes widening a fraction. He whispered, "Are you the grim reaper?"

She shook her head. "No. I'm *a* grim reaper."

Chapter 5

Silas stared at Tessa, his throat working as though a bunch of words were fighting each other to be the first one out of his mouth. None of them won. He remained silent.

Tessa's phone buzzed. She pulled it out of her pocket, and her brow furrowed as she scrolled down the list of pop-ups on the screen.

"My phone's been blowing up," she muttered.

During all the running and screaming and siren wailing, she hadn't heard or felt it buzzing. She had a bunch of missed calls and texts from the office telling her to get there for a meeting immediately. The last one from Gloria, said, "SOS. Get here now."

"What on earth? Silas, I don't know what's going on, but there's some kind of emergency at the office."

Silas didn't reach for the door handle. "What did you just say?"

She held up the phone. "Work is being weird. Well, weirder." Usually, it was a laid-back office just as long as the reaps got done.

Silas shook his head. "Not that. Before. I mean, I know what you said. You said you're a grim reaper. But I was just kidding when I suggested that. I mean kind of. I did think something supernatural was afoot." Another head shake that sent his hair to flapping over troubled eyes. "But how is it possible to be that? If you don't work for an assisted suicide organization, then what is it? Some kind of government thing? Are you an agent of some sort?"

"Sort of. I swear I'll explain all of this to you. Tonight. Right now, I have to get to work."

"Right. Your work. Grim reaping or whatever." Finally, some color flooded into Silas's too-pale face. With it, anger floated across his features. He reached for the door handle.

"It's complicated," Tessa said.

"I'm sure."

Tessa's phone buzzed again. She winced.

"I don't know what's going on here, but I'm not sure I can be associated with it." He stabbed a finger toward Tessa's phone. "You do what you have to do. Maybe I'll be around tonight to hear your explanation—and maybe I won't."

He jumped out of Linda before Tessa could say anything else, slamming the door behind him. He stalked to his pickup truck, got in, and pulled away.

Part of Tessa wanted to wheel the car around and follow him back to Mist River Manor. She could explain everything right that moment and smooth things over before he could stew over it all afternoon, getting angrier and more frightened. Because she was sure part of his reaction was fear.

If she put herself in his shoes, she would be scared. She imagined herself following her boyfriend to a mansion, only to find him standing in a room with a man whose lifeless body lay in a bowl of cereal. She shuddered. Terror would probably be right at the top of the list of emotions she'd be having. Especially if the boyfriend's explanation for the whole thing was that he was a grim reaper.

Tessa's phone buzzed again. Whatever this was, it truly must be an emergency. She groaned before pulling the car onto the street and heading away from Silas and toward the façade that was the Cooper's Life Insurance building.

Her mind wasn't really on the driving. It lurched back and forth between the situation with Silas and Artemis Green's contention that someone had poisoned him. Before she knew it, and without having worked through either of the problems her mind had been chewing on, Tessa arrived at work.

She sprinted across the broken sidewalk and through the front door and then stopped short—short of crashing into another reaper, Jake. The lobby was full of people. Gloria and Cheryl were there, as were the other two reapers who worked at their agency and the secretary.

There was a thermos of coffee and an open box of donuts on the counter above the secretary's desk. But there were no regular donuts left, only some sort of cream filled and a bear claw. Neither of which Tessa fancied. Good thing she'd had cereal. But the thought of cereal took her mind back to Mr. Green.

Six necks swiveled and twelve eyes focused on Tessa, who felt like their gazes physically pinned her to the closed door behind her. "Um. Hi!" She followed up her overly perky greeting with a toddler-like wave. "Sorry I'm late."

Cheryl rolled her eyes. "Where were you? Your assignment was over ages ago."

"I was . . . well, my car wouldn't start." It wasn't anyone's business that she'd been caught in a reap by her almost-boyfriend and then had to escape the situation, dragging him along, before the cops and ambulance showed up.

Okay, maybe it was her mom-boss's business. But she could read about it later in Tessa's report. That was another thing she'd never have expected going into this job—that grim reaping came with paperwork.

The way Cheryl's lips thinned let Tessa know her mother was onto her lie. But she didn't push it. "If everyone's ready, let's move into the conference room. I've called this meeting to announce a few changes."

Relieved that her mom's gaze shifted to scoot everyone in the lobby to the adjacent meeting room, Tessa took the opportunity to stand next to her friend, Gloria, who bumped her elbow and grinned as they passed the threshold to the next room.

Cheryl continued, even before they were all in their seats, "I received word yesterday that our district manager, April, is leaving her position to take over the western district manager position. She'll be moving from Chicago to LA within the week."

Interesting. That didn't seem like a promotion to Tessa but more of a lateral move. Maybe April fancied getting out of Chicago.

"As such, April's position was vacant, and I have been promoted to fill it." The centimeter that the corners of her lips twitched upward was Cheryl's only outward indication of pride at the turn of events.

Around Tessa, people broke into applause, and she hurried to join in. "Will you be moving to Chicago?" she blurted out.

Cheryl's smile widened. "Are you hoping for the answer to be yes or no?" But, immediately following the question, she waved a hand. "Don't answer that. I don't want to know. I think I'll be staying here in Mist River, for the most part. More traveling will be required of me than before, but for now, this will be my home office."

A chorus of congratulations and muttered well-wishes rang through the conference room. When it died down, Cheryl said, "Of course, this unexpected promotion meant my previous position was empty. But not for long. I'm happy to announce that, this morning, I requested that Gloria fill the job, and she accepted."

There was more applause. Stunned, Tessa turned to her friend who beamed. "Thanks, everyone," she said, raising her hands in the air and giving herself a couple little claps too. Then she dropped her arms. "Now. Party's over. Everybody get back to work. No slacking!" She delivered the directive in a teasing tone.

The other reapers stopped by to shake Gloria's hand at the door before heading out.

Now, Tessa realized that the conference room had been retrofitted. All of Cheryl's things were here, even the framed Glamour Shot of her from middle school with an abundance of pink blush and heavy blue eye shadow. Had everyone seen that?

Soon, Tessa was alone with Gloria in the lobby. "So." She crossed her arms. "Since you're my boss now, does that mean we can't have movie and ice cream marathons at my place anymore? Or makeup tutorials at yours?" Tessa tried to keep her tone light and teasing, but she was actually concerned.

Everybody knew that when one friend was promoted over another, it usually caused a chasm to open between the two.

The dynamics of the relationship changed, and the friendship as it was before died.

But Gloria shook her head. "Don't worry about that. We're buds, and this isn't going to have an impact on that." She smiled, her perfectly applied ruby lipstick glistening as it caught the overhead light. "I'm planning to approach this job a little differently than your mom did. I see myself as more of a mentor than a boss."

"Oh! That's great. Because I'm in dire need of some mentoring right now." Tessa wrinkled her nose. "I need help. Badly."

"Business or personal?" Gloria asked.

Tessa thought for a second. "A little of both," she decided.

Gloria tipped her head back. "Ah. Landlord trouble, right? Come on into my office, and we'll hash it out."

She'd already moved all her things into Cheryl's old office. The only things that remained the same were the desk and the chair. Gloria wasn't quite as neat as Cheryl. She seemed to have picked up everything off her old desk and put it on this one without any thought of giving it a new place. She had a few plants, one in the window and two in odd positions on the bookshelf.

Once they were safely inside with the door shut, Tessa's new boss said, "Hit me with it," and made a *come on* motion with her hand.

"So, Silas followed me to my assignment this morning. I'm not sure what he saw—not all of it. But enough to understand the guy was alive when I arrived and dead when I left."

Gloria let out a low whistle and plopped into her office chair. "That guy is persistent."

"Yeah. And he's good at tailing people. He's done it to me twice now, and I didn't realize it either time. You know, we should really get better training when we become reapers, shouldn't we? Like some kind of law enforcement drills or something." Tessa crossed the room to look at some framed pictures on a bookshelf. Gloria with people who were probably her parents in front of the Cinderella castle at Disney World, Gloria in a cap and gown, and Gloria hugging another woman around the waist, all smiles. She pointed at the last one. "Who's that?"

"We don't have money for more training," Gloria said without answering the question. "And, besides, people don't usually follow us around. Your guy is only doing that because he's specifically interested in you and what you're doing."

Tessa huffed and paced around the perimeter of the office. It felt odd to her—familiar but not. "Okay, so what do I do? I get the feeling he isn't going to let this drop. He's just going to keep following me around, trying to figure out what's going on."

"He knows you're not telling him the whole truth," Gloria agreed. "He can feel it. And it's not fair to him to try and develop a romantic relationship with him that's based on trust when you aren't really being trustworthy."

Tessa glared at her friend. "I'm trustworthy!"

"You're lying to him. Every day. That's untrustworthy if I ever saw it." She tapped her fingertips on the desk calendar in front of her. "Come clean."

"I am. I will. I wasn't *trying* to be untrustworthy," Tessa argued. "I was trying to keep us a secret. Isn't that what I was supposed to do?"

Gloria shrugged an elegant shoulder. "Eh."

"Eh? Eh? What do you mean eh?"

"I mean, we aren't superheroes or something. What's the worst that could happen if folks know we exist?"

Tessa's scowl deepened. "I don't know. Imprisonment? Lab experiments? I mean, I assume people might decide we're killers. Like no one would die if we weren't around to reap them or something."

Gloria rolled her eyes. "This isn't a movie. Nobody cares. Besides, I'm not suggesting we out ourselves to the whole world. I'm saying you should tell your boyfriend. There's a big difference."

"But what if he tells other people?"

"Ask him not to. Trust is a two-way street." She leaned forward to rest her elbows on the desk. "Girl, he's into you. You're into him. If you're honest and lay it out for him, then ask him to keep it to himself. He will. Silas cares about you."

Tessa pursed her lips, considering. It did sound like the best course of action.

Gloria winked. "Go talk to your boyfriend. It'll be okay."

And, just like that, Tessa found that she was out of arguments. Gloria was right. "Fine," she said. "You're my boss now, so I guess I have to do what you say." She headed to the door but stopped short and said over her shoulder, "Thanks for the pep talk."

Gloria made a shooing motion. "Go on. Get it done so you can focus on your job. I don't need any reapers who aren't fully focused on their work around here." She softened the bossy words with a grin.

Tessa smiled back and left, her steps feeling lighter than when she'd arrived.

Her friend and newly appointed boss was right. Silas did seem to care about her. And it wasn't fair to him to withhold basic information about herself.

She'd already told him she was a reaper. Now, she could explain what that meant. He'd have to understand why she had to lie before. Then, they could move on, and she could be herself with him.

That sounded amazing.

Tessa drove a little faster than she should have to the apartment building, marveling over how smoothly Linda was running now. That Silas sure was magical when it came to mechanics.

The excitement she felt over coming clean about her job warred with a little bit of nervousness as she pulled into the lot and parked. Tessa reminded herself of what Gloria had said—that everything would be fine.

But before she got out of the car, her attention was captured by people coming out of the lobby of Mist River Manor.

And she knew it wasn't true. Things weren't going to be fine at all.

Because Silas was in handcuffs, each elbow held by a cop as they propelled him toward a waiting police cruiser.

Chapter 6

Tessa stood in the parking lot wondering what to do. Should she follow the officers and Silas to the police station? After all, this was all her fault. Okay, maybe not *all* her fault. Silas had made the choice to follow her. But he didn't know what he was getting himself into. And she could've done a better job explaining away her job.

Or she could've told him the truth from the beginning. It seemed like such a simple solution now.

It only took a moment's thought to give up on the idea of following him to the station—she knew they'd spend at least an hour booking and probably questioning him. It was possible they'd let him go home after that but, if not, they'd put him in a cell to await a court date. And that wouldn't likely occur for a day or two. Then Silas would go in front of a judge, who would decide whether he had to stay in jail or could be let out on bond.

This wasn't like visiting a patient in a hospital. Even then, she wasn't his family. She wasn't even really his girlfriend. Silas was incommunicado with only one phone call. And she doubted he'd waste it on her. There was very little to nothing Tessa was able to do besides get in everybody's way and annoy them.

So, shoulders slumped, she trudged through the apartment building. She was already dreaming about drowning her sorrows in a half-gallon of ice cream and hoping the streaming service she shared with her friend Abi in a different apartment wasn't overloaded and would work for her. She was dreaming of a comedy—something to keep her mind off Silas's predicament.

Before she got to her apartment, another door opened. Mrs. Cross swayed in the doorway, without her cane. She wore a floor length housecoat and a cream-colored bandana wrapped around her hair. "Come in here, girl," she croaked, reaching out to grab Tessa's elbow and then swaying even harder.

Tessa automatically stiffened her arm to stabilize the woman.

Taken aback, she wondered if Mrs. Cross had been watching for Tessa through the peephole.

Oh, yeah, that's not creepy or anything.

"What can I do for you?" Tessa kept her tone light, even though she was irritated about the probable spying.

"I want to talk to you." Mrs. Cross peered through thick glasses at Tessa. Her tone, as always, was gruff. Like the schoolteacher no one ever messed with, even though she was small and fragile enough to simply push over. No one would ever dare do that. She was the type who inspired fear and respect, even though she didn't have the physical oomph to back it up.

"Okay," Tessa stammered. She cast one last longing look toward her own apartment before crossing the threshold into Mrs. Cross's.

The lady's apartment looked like one would expect the dwelling space of a single woman in their eighties to look. It was decorated in country style, with blue and white flowered fabric for curtains and a matching pattern on the upholstery. Knick-knacks covered every available surface, and dirty teacups and plates sat precariously on top of other items, threatening to pitch off to their metaphorical deaths at any moment.

But even more than the clutter and countrified décor, the thing that stood out about the home was its strong odor. Tessa's nose twitched, and she longed to rub it but had a pretty good idea that Mrs. Cross would notice and call her out on it. Then what would she say? Somehow, "I'm sorry, but this place reeks," didn't seem advisable.

And the scent wasn't bad, per se. It smelled like orange and cinnamon and reminded Tessa of the mall during Christmastime. Except it was stronger. Much, much stronger. In addition to the twitchy nose, Tessa began to suffer a low-grade burning in her eyes, which watered in response.

Great. I need to figure out how to make this quick.

Mrs. Cross lowered herself onto a tattered brown armchair with a crooked footrest that indicated it didn't go up and down anymore.

Tessa glanced around. The only places left for her to sit were either on a blue-flowered loveseat or a sofa, both of which were covered with heavy plastic protector sheets.

She hesitated, then chose the sofa. When she sat, it creaked and croaked under her weight. Gingerly, she chose a position that wasn't quite comfortable and then froze, hoping to keep the plastic quiet. It reminded her of visiting her grandmother's house as a child. She'd never felt relaxed there either.

Too late, Tessa realized her mistake. A simmering pot of liquid potpourri sat bubbling away on an end table inches away from her right elbow, emitting the nearly overpowering Christmas odor. Tessa's eyes redoubled their effort to protect her from the horrendous scent by watering harder.

"Make yourself comfortable, girl," Mrs. Cross rumbled. "You look like a giraffe trying to sit on its rear end like a dog."

Tessa's mind helpfully produced a mental image of that colorful description for her, and she laughed. "No, no. I'm not uncomfortable at all. This is just like home. Thanks for inviting me in—um, why did you invite me in, again?"

"I wanted to tell you about our landlord!"

"You did? You do?" Tessa's already troubled eyes twitched slightly.

"I was listening to the police scanner earlier, and I heard the whole thing. I wouldn't've believed it if I hadn't heard it with my own ears." She wrinkled her nose, giving Tessa a moment's hope that she was bothered by the strong odor too and would authorize the bubbler's unplugging. But she just went on, "Actually, I didn't hear with my *own* ears. I had to turn my hearing aids way up to catch it. But, even using those cheaters, I know what they said."

Tessa leaned forward so her elbows were resting on her knees. "Really? What did you hear?"

"For one, I heard that my old boss Artemis Green died this morning." She shook her head, and a pink foam curler popped out from under the woman's beige-colored bandanna.

"I'm sorry to hear you lost an, um, employer."

"Oh, I'd say he was much more than that. I'd say we were friends—as good as one can be with their boss."

That stung a little. Tessa wanted to believe the dynamic between she and Gloria would stay the same. Granted, she didn't know what type of work Mrs. Cross did. She doubted it was reaping souls.

"Well, I'm sorry you lost a friend. What happened to him?" Not only did Tessa think it was a good idea to play along with the conversation to keep Mrs. Cross happy, but she was also hoping to figure out what everyone thought Mr. Green might've died from.

"Yes, yes. He and I go way back." Mrs. Cross disregarded the question, choosing instead to languish in her memories. She sat back in her chair, her voice smoothing out from her usual cackle as she reminisced. "I used to work at his house, you know. I did the cleaning there, and then I was in the kitchen for a while. But I'm horrible in the kitchen, and, out of self-defense for his taste buds, Artemis quickly moved me out to work with horses."

"They're gorgeous," Tessa said offhand, remembering those she'd seen while hiding in the grounds at Artemis's house. She realized her mistake. "I mean horses in general. I, uh, I love them."

Mrs. Cross squinted but seemed to believe the quick correction. "Yes. They're very fine creatures. And Artemis only brought the best specimens into his barn. He never rode himself, but he liked to have them around for his kids and grandkids and their friends. Most of the time, the horses lived like kings, getting the finest food and veterinary care.

"Two wipe-downs every day in the very best brushes. Every once in a while, one of them would get saddled up and ridden for half an hour or so, but the rest of the time, their lives were their own. Anyway, I got to know Artemis pretty well during all that time."

"You did?"

"While he wasn't a rider, you could usually find him somewhere near the barn. He loved the outdoors. Plus, I think he just liked to get out of the house, and away from Mrs. Green."

"Oh?" Tessa leaned in closer. She tried to put her question delicately. "Was she not very nice?"

"It wasn't like that, dear. She was often sick and bedridden. Some sort of autoimmune disease. Spent her time indoors with her calligraphy. I think it pained Artemis to see her that way."

"Oh." Tessa rubbed at her reddening eyes.

"But like I was saying, he loved the outdoors. He and my husband used to play golf every once in a while—Artemis would invite Stanley and pay for everything. He was a very generous man."

"It certainly sounds like it. How long did you work there?"

She pondered the question as though trying to read the answer on an imaginary sheet of paper. "Well. This was years ago. But let's see. I was in the kitchen for about six months before Sky took over my position and I went to the barn. And I was in the barn for about fifteen years, I think."

"Sky?"

"A flower child, they used to call them. She was a much better chef than I was but kind of a brat. I've always been surprised Artemis didn't kick her out on her behind. But he never did. I believe her daughter Lark works there now, actually. In the same position, not in the barn." She re-focused and nodded curtly. "It was nice out there. Got to be alone most of the time. The only people I reported to were Artemis and then Nathaniel."

"Nathaniel?"

"Artemis's son-in-law. Real piece of work, he is. Never did a lick of work in his life—only real decision he ever made was to marry into the Green family wealth—but likes to act like the king of the castle. He'd come into the barn and stir up a bunch of dust about one thing or another and then leave again."

"What did you do about that?" These all seemed like more likely culprits than Silas. Tessa wished the police had stopped to interview Mrs. Cross.

"I learned to bite my tongue when he arrived and ignore everything he'd said once he was gone again." She snorted. "Sometimes you have to do that in your professional life, you know. Let the boss think he's in charge but do things the right way when he isn't looking. Makes everyone happy."

Tessa wanted to argue. To tell Mrs. Cross it was stupid to do that. That you should be able to tell your boss you had a better way of doing something and accept the credit when it went well. But she swallowed the words. Mrs. Cross was past her working days, and it wasn't going to do any good to argue with the elderly woman now.

Mrs. Cross clucked her tongue. "Well, anyway, Nathaniel will probably take over the place now. Likely, he'll run it into disrepair. That is if his wife, Hannah, lets him. Because Artemis is gone now, and old Mrs. Green is in no shape to do much of anything."

"That's terrible." Tessa wanted to console Mrs. Cross. But even more, she wanted to make a getaway. The smell was that bad.

"According to the scanner, he died in his breakfast cereal," Mrs. Cross continued. "When the police got there, they didn't have any reason to think there was any foul play involved. It looked like he just had a heart attack and keeled over while he was eating breakfast. But, of course, they fanned out and looked around the place anyway. That's when one of the officers found a bottle of Grime Slayer. You know the stuff, girl?"

Tessa nodded. She watched enough late-night TV that the jingle for the heavy-duty cleaner with the tagline "It's murder on muck," got stuck in her head weekly. She started singing it, and Mrs. Cross joined in.

When they were done, the elderly woman chuckled. "Anyway, it's no surprise they'd have cleaner around—Artemis insisted on a spotless home. But the stuff was in the kitchen, right on the counter next to the spot where someone would've made Artemis's breakfast. That's when the cops got a little suspicious, and one of them asked the staff to see the security footage of the house."

Tessa almost smacked her forehead with a palm but remembered at the last minute that she shouldn't act like she knew anything about the situation. So, she smacked her forehead internally.

Of course. The security cameras.

She'd known where to look for them and how to get around them at an angle where she wouldn't be caught on film, but Silas wouldn't have been thinking about any of that. He probably just barged straight through their field of view. "But why would Silas be at Mr. Green's house?"

Mrs. Cross scoffed. "How should I know? I thought he was a very fine boy. I even gave him some money from my lottery winnings." She shook her head again, more violently this time, and two more rollers escaped from their bandana fabric captor. "I can't believe I was so wrong about him. I'm usually a fine judge of character. But he was at Mr. Green's house, skulking around. So, the cops got a search warrant."

Tessa nodded along, thinking it couldn't get any worse. There was no way there'd be anything linking Silas to Artemis Green's death here at the apartment complex.

"They came here to Mist River Manor and searched Silas's apartment and his pickup truck." Her sharp eyes met Tessa's, and Mrs. Cross scowled. "They found an open bottle of Grime Slayer right in that boy's truck cab. I just can't believe he wasn't smart enough to hide it better."

"Hide it? You mean, you think Silas actually had something to do with this man's death?"

"Well, of course I do. And I'm no slouch in the mystery solving department, girl. I watch all the BBC mysteries of them all the time, plus I get my Agatha Christie and Sherlock Holmes from the library. This is an open and shut case if I ever heard one."

"I'm not sure . . ."

But Mrs. Cross interrupted Tessa. "Now, girl, I know you had the hots for our landlord, but you're just going to have to give up on that idea."

The hots? Tessa had to hold in a laugh at the words that seemed so mismatched to the woman in front of her.

Mrs. Cross continued, "The boy's a murderer. We'll have to get a new landlord in here and you're just going to have to find a new love interest." She scooched to the end of her chair, grabbed a cane leaning on the coffee table in front of her, and struggled to her feet.

Tessa jumped up, setting the plastic to crackling, and offered a hand to the elderly lady. But Mrs. Cross slapped it away. "I think I can get around in my own home. Now, I guess I'll be having my nap now. I just wanted to make sure you understood what that man of yours is all about. Tread carefully, now. Don't get pulled into trouble yourself."

She headed toward the back of the apartment, not bothering to walk Tessa to the door, and disappeared into the hallway without another word.

Tessa hurried out of the apartment, closing the door firmly behind her, and drew in a deep breath, as though Mrs. Cross's assessment of Mr. Green's death was bad air that she could clear out by inhaling fresh oxygen.

It didn't work. But her nose and eyes did appreciate the gift of potpourri-free air.

Tessa wiped her eyes on a sleeve and then trudged toward her apartment again.

Mrs. Cross might think it was an open and shut case against Silas, but she was wrong. It was anything but that. Still, it was highly unlikely that the investigators, a jury, or a judge would see it Tessa's way. Not without more information, anyway. They would see Silas on the security camera footage and the cleaner in his truck that matched the one found in Artemis's kitchen.

They'd consider it open and shut too.

A war of emotions was taking place inside Tessa's chest. She felt guilty. If it wasn't for her, Silas wouldn't be in this mess.

But she also felt angry. Couldn't he just have trusted her? She'd never done anything to warrant him not believing what she said and following her around the way he had—twice!

Now he'd gone and gotten himself in a whole heap of trouble, and it was going to be up to Tessa to try and get him out.

Only she had no idea how to do that. Frustration rolled over and through her like a giant tidal wave.

Then it hit her, and she groaned. The only way to get Silas out of the mess was to figure out who *had* killed Artemis Green. Because not only did the cops think there was foul play involved, but the man himself had too.

"I see your groan and raise you a deep sigh." Abi leaned against Tessa's apartment door. She grinned and held up both hands to show Tessa what she held. "I figured that was how you'd be feeling after Mrs. Cross yanked you into her horribly stinky apartment. She did the same to me—to tell me what happened to Silas. So, I brought wine and ice cream to help you feel better."

Tessa thought about sending her friend home. But there was nothing she could do to help Silas right then. So, she forced a smile and reached around Abi to unlock the door. "That sounds perfect. Come on in."

Chapter 7

"Tessa Randolph, get your booty in my office immediately!"

For a second, Tessa thought she had transported back to when her mother was in charge. But it wasn't Cheryl yelling for her presence—it was Gloria, who'd stuck her head out to bark the order and then pulled it back into her office.

In trouble, yet again. New boss. Same problems.

Tessa shuffled in and shut the door behind her when Gloria jabbed a finger at it. Whatever Gloria wanted, Tessa hoped it didn't take long. As soon as she'd woken up that morning, she'd been anxious to start her new side gig—figuring out who had killed Artemis Green. Only then could she get Silas out of trouble.

Her reaper app hadn't shown any appointments, but a text shimmered on her screen, ordering her to head to the Cooper's Life Insurance building. She'd barely crossed the threshold when Gloria yelled for her.

Now, Gloria's mouth was a firm line as she tilted her head and examined Tessa.

"What's up?" Tessa ventured.

"You didn't tell me the reap Silas followed you on was for *the* Artemis Green." Gloria's eyes, lids covered with a gorgeous shade of fuchsia eyeshadow, were wide as they pinned Tessa with a hard look. "That was a pretty important bit of information to leave out."

Tessa shrugged. "Was it? Sorry. I didn't know who *the* Artemis Green was until yesterday. Actually, I still really don't get why he's such a big deal."

Gloria gave her head a little shake, setting her braids to bouncing. "I thought everybody in Mist River knew Mr. Green. I don't know how you grew up here and *didn't* know about him." She lowered herself into an office chair and stared at Tessa, her expression bordering on reproachful.

"I don't know. I just never had a lot of contact with rich old guys." Tessa sat on the edge of Gloria's desk. "And it's not like he's the only rich old guy who lives over in that area of town. So, why is this particular dude so important?"

"Well, for one, he's a self-made multimillionaire. As in, he started with nothing and built himself up. Which is unlike most of the other rich folk in this town. How they keep living on old money, I'll never understand. And second, because I said multimillionaire. And I don't just mean a few millions—I mean hundreds of millions."

"Wow. That's pretty interesting. How'd he make that kind of money from nothing?"

Gloria wrinkled her nose. "I don't know. Something boring like the stock market or banking or real estate or perhaps all three." She waved a hand, dismissing the importance of that particular bit of information. "But, like I said, he's a big deal, and his lawyers aren't going to spare any expense trying to get Silas convicted of his murder."

Tessa winced and stretched her neck, first to one side and then the other. "Okay, I've been thinking about this. The only way to get Silas out of this is to figure out who really did poison Mr. Green. Can't we just look at his file and find out who killed him?"

But Gloria was shaking her head before the full question was out of Tessa's mouth. "Nope, it doesn't work that way. Our job is to escort souls to the other side of the veil, not to worry about how or why they died. It's just not the sort of thing that's included in our record keeping." She pushed off the armrests, getting to her feet. "Come on. I'm going to be mentoring you through your reaps today."

Gloria headed for the door. Tessa admired the floor-length maxi dress her friend wore, which was the same shade of fuchsia as her eyeshadow.

"I've been reaping for months. Why do I need mentoring now?" Tessa hopped off the desk and followed Gloria into the lobby.

Gloria cast a smirk over her shoulder. "Because you're a slow learner."

Tessa's jaw dropped and she stopped walking for a second and then had to hurry to catch back up. "I am not! There's just been a lot of weird stuff going on since I came on, that's all. I mean, it isn't like everything's been routine or easy with the reaps."

"Actually, it's my opinion that everything *has* been routine and boring, but you've been inserting some drama." Gloria made a beeline for her car, and Tessa followed without arguing.

Gloria's ride was much more reliable than Linda.

"I'm not dramatic."

Gloria's cheeks puffed out like a chipmunk's. And then she burst into high-pitched laughter. "Really? You're going to take that route? Honey, you bring more drama with you than Hollywood celebrities bring to the red carpet. It's one thing after another with you.

"First, you lose a soul, then you exchange one soul for another, then you're involved in a bunch of improper reaps at the convention." She pointed a finger at Tessa's nose. "I'm telling you, *you're* the one bringing the madness."

Tessa got in the car and put on her seatbelt. Then she crossed her arms and huffed. "Okay, I lost the soul. That much was my fault. But all the stuff that happened in Miami—that had nothing to do with me. I was just along for the ride. In fact, I'm the one who got it all figured out and cleared up. You should be thanking me instead of..." Tessa waved a hand in the air aimlessly. "Whatever this is."

Gloria put the car in reverse and eased out of the spot. "Relax. All I'm going to do is show you a couple of tricks of the trade. It's not any kind of statement about what kind of job you're doing. It has more to do with me taking over and making things ... you know, the way I want them."

Now, that actually didn't sound bad. Cheryl's management style, while standoffish, was fairly intense. She liked things to be just so and didn't hesitate to micromanage to get them that way.

Maybe Gloria would be a little more lenient. And, if nothing else, she'd been reaping for a lot longer than Tessa and would have some tricks up her sleeve. Tessa was interested in learning all the tricks possible. Even after the flubs and dangerous situations Tessa had been put into since she became a reaper, she really did love the job. She wanted not only to keep at it but also to do a great job. She just had to figure out how to get Silas out of trouble first.

Gloria glanced at her. "You're pouting again. It's about your boyfriend, isn't it?"

"He's not my boyfriend," Tessa replied automatically, following up with, "I'm serious—he really isn't my boyfriend.

We had an argument the night before Artemis Green's reap. And Silas was really upset after he followed me and saw what happened. He didn't understand. He thought our agency was some sort of assisted suicide thing. I never had a chance to explain it before he was arrested."

"Okay, well, that's not good. But don't worry. You'll get it straightened out and hottie landlord will be your boyfriend again." The grin on Gloria's face could only be described as impish.

"That reminds me. You're always trying to get involved in my love life—giving me advice and all that on what to do with Silas. I don't ever get to hear about *your* love life. In Miami, you said you do have one. So, what gives? Who are you dating?"

Gloria kept her eyes on the road. "I date lots of people," she said cryptically. "But I've been seeing someone a little bit more seriously the last couple of weeks." She paused.

Tessa could see her friend chewing the inside of her lip, like she was nervous. What did she have to be nervous about? "Okay, spill it. Tell me about this mysterious person."

"There's not much to tell." She checked the side mirror, even though there was no reason to because she wasn't changing lanes. Then she spoke in a fast rush of words. "Her name's Ella. If you're nice to me, maybe I'll let you meet her."

Her. That was something Tessa hadn't known about Gloria. But it clicked into place in her mind fast, filling in a piece of knowledge that had been missing. "That sounds great. I can't wait to meet her." Tessa smiled. "Ooh, does she like Thai food? I've been dying to see if that new place downtown is any good."

Gloria finally glanced at Tessa. "Thanks," she said softly.

"For what?"

"For not being weird about it."

Tessa scowled. "Why would I be weird about it? I don't care who you date. I just want you to be happy. And to stay out of *my* love life." She jabbed Gloria's arm lightly with her elbow.

Gloria snorted. "Never gonna happen."

She twisted the wheel, pulling the car into Mist River Hospital's parking lot. "You need all the help you can get with that love life of yours. Just consider me your personal relationship guru. You should be paying me a salary."

Gloria threw the car in park and hopped out before Tessa could get a word in edgewise.

"Great," she muttered, following more slowly.

At first, Tessa thought she'd missed Gloria somehow. She was nowhere to be seen between the front of the car and the hospital. Then she heard the sound of the car trunk popping open.

Gloria began digging in the trunk, so Tessa joined her there. A lot like her desk, it was a mess. Her trunk was like a middle schooler's locker at the end of the year.

"Why are we here?" She jabbed a thumb toward the squat gray hospital building. Mist River was such a small town it was a wonder they had one, but it served the whole western part of the county. Recently, a big out-of-state company bought it, which was a huge scandal, but they'd upgraded the facilities and raised all the workers' compensation, so that shut everyone up quickly.

"There's a reap for you in there," Gloria said, tossing bags and papers to the edges of the trunk until she said, "Aha," and pulled a small green duffel back to the top of the pile. She unzipped and rifled through it for a minute before pulling out a pair of light blue scrubs. "Put these on."

Tessa scowled again, but Gloria made a face that said she shouldn't argue. Tessa pulled the shirt over her own fitted T-shirt.

"Good thing I'm wearing leggings," she muttered as she stepped into the scrub pants. If she'd worn jeans, she would have had to make herself into a pretzel to change in the back seat.

But Gloria wasn't paying attention—she was still digging in the duffel bag. "Where is it? I know it was here last time!"

"Maybe you should clean out your trunk," Tessa suggested.

Gloria shot her a glare. "I can't. This is everything I may need to blend in anywhere. Your trunk should look just like this."

Tessa frowned.

"Okay. Maybe not *just* like this. But this stuff is important."

It made sense. Having scrubs or overalls or a wig or whatever would definitely make it easier to look inconspicuous on a reap. Tessa made a note to visit the local thrift shops and see what she could stock up on.

"Bingo!" Gloria held up a card attached to a brown lanyard, which she handed to Tessa with a triumphant smile. "Here you go."

Tessa accepted the item and turned the card over to examine it. "There's nothing on this. What is it?"

Gloria pointed at the card. "*That* is your ticket into any place you'll need to go to reap." She re-zipped the duffel bag and closed the trunk, then leaned on the bumper. "It's a universal badge that has some Grim Reaper magic in it. Becomes whatever you need it to be."

Tessa turned it over again, but it still just looked like a plain laminated white card to her. "What am I missing?"

"Walk toward the hospital. Watch the card."

With a shrug, Tessa put the lanyard around her neck and then did as Gloria directed. When she was within about twenty feet of the hospital, Gloria called, "Check the badge."

Tessa pulled the card up to examine it and pulled in a breath when she saw it now showed a picture of her, in scrubs, and proclaimed her to be Nurse Lottie Swan.

"Wow," she breathed, heading back toward Gloria. In front of her eyes, the picture on the badge became fuzzy and then vanished completely as she walked away from the hospital. "So, this is, like, an all-access pass, huh?"

"Within reason," Gloria said. She held up her cell phone and wagged it in the air. "I just assigned you the reap of Mrs. Samantha Hughes, room 323 inside. But yes. That card will act as a badge or pass key or whatever you need. Cheryl didn't think you were ready for it. I do."

Tessa rolled her eyes. "Figures she'd think I wasn't capable. She's never given me credit for anything."

Gloria gave her a nudge toward the building. "I'm your boss and your love life consultant, not your therapist. Get in there and escort Mrs. Hughes over, will you? We don't have all day."

Tessa stuck her tongue out at her friend but went toward the hospital.

The badge worked perfectly. No one gave her a second glance as she walked around the hospital like she belonged there, straight into Mrs. Hughes' restricted visits room.

When she was finished, she found Gloria still leaning on the trunk of her car. "How'd it go?"

"Fine. What's next?"

"Another reap. This one's at the chemical plant. Don't worry—one of us is prepared. I have a white jumper suit for you. You can give that thing another whirl." She pointed at the card around Tessa's neck. "You'll need it to get past the guard at the front desk and then into the lab room where Don Stempin is."

"Fine. Let's go. How many of these do we have today, anyway? I want to work on the Artemis Green case."

"A few." They got into the car, and Gloria started it up. "What are you going to do, anyway? Where are you going to start the investigation?"

"I don't know. But I was thinking maybe I could do something like I did with Chet Sanborn's family. You know how I went over there and talked to them about the life insurance policy? I could go to Mr. Green's house and say I'm there about his policy. Maybe I'll be able to talk to some people, get some information."

Gloria scoffed and shook her head. "No way. His family would never believe he'd taken out insurance from a run-down agency like Cooper's."

Disappointment shot through Tessa, but she knew her friend was right. "Okay, well, that was my only bright idea. Do you have any?"

Gloria winked. "We're just going to have to get creative."

Chapter 8

"What do you mean by *creative*?" Tessa studied Gloria's profile as her friend drove.

"Let's just say a promotion wasn't all I received this morning." The tiny smile on Gloria's lips reminded Tessa of a kid who'd spotted a present with her name on it.

"What do you mean? What else did you get?"

As though she'd been dying to say it for hours, Gloria burst out, "I was endowed with Lee Stuart's reaper ability! This girl can turn invisible."

Tessa felt her eyes pop open. This was big news.

When the earth's population had gotten to the point where the original Grim Reaper was hopping busy, he'd decided he wanted to retire, take it easy, and lounge around on beaches to drink coconutty cocktails. So, he'd come up with the idea of reaper agencies and allowed small bits of his power to be used by others. Most reapers just got the actual reaping power—the ability to open a path across the veil and escort souls over. But some select few also received other secrets of the original reaper. Tessa had been gifted the ability to conjure an actual scythe, which she had used only once so far.

"I can't believe they gave you invisibility! That's amazing."

Gloria's head bobbed as though she were listening to music. Tessa had never seen her so excited. "Yep. I guess Mr. Blade noticed me helping you at the convention and arranged for Lee's secret to pass to me." She winked. "This has been one of the best days of my life. When I was a kid playing superhero, invisibility was *always* my choice. And now it's real—not just me hiding under a blanket."

She giggled like the little girl in the memory. "Of course, I'm not supposed to go around all willy-nilly, just becoming invisible for no reason. Luckily, you've provided me with the perfect excuse!"

"I have?" Tessa wrinkled her nose for a second. "Wait, this is what you meant by getting creative? You're going to use it?"

Gloria turned onto the road leading to Artemis Green's suburb. "We are. Let's see if we can find anything out from the source."

They parked about a quarter mile down the road and walked toward Mr. Green's driveway. Tessa could feel Gloria's excitement increase as they got closer. Her arms shook with anticipation, and a smile stayed etched on her face.

Before they got into view of the security gate at the end of the driveway, Gloria stopped short and grabbed Tessa's arm. "Okay. I'm obviously a novice at this, but I think if we stay in contact, I can extend the invisibility to you."

Tessa eyed her friend for a second. "You know, my mom never would do this. When you said you were going to be a different kind of boss from her, you weren't kidding."

Gloria shrugged, and her eyebrows danced upward. "If you want to forget about this, we can go back to the office, and I can write you up for carelessness on the job. You know, for letting Silas follow you on a reap. That would be more bosserly, right?"

"For one, that's not a word." Tessa rolled her eyes. "For two, I can do without the write-up. But are you sure you want to do this so soon after your promotion? I'm pretty sure it's not something upper management would get behind. In fact, I'm positive Mom would let the police sort it out. She'd say it's not our problem and that I should keep my head down and do my work."

"You do have a little bit of Cheryl in you," Gloria said. "I can see it now. And you're probably right. I shouldn't be doing this. It's a big risk."

"But?"

"But the police seem pretty convinced they got their man already. I think if they're going to do any *sorting* out, it's only going to be to drum up more evidence to support their conclusion. They aren't going to be looking for another suspect."

"You're right." Tessa felt bad about bringing her friend into this. What if something happened—what if her mom did find out about this? Both she and Gloria would get fired. She couldn't stand for that.

The trepidation showed on her face because Gloria said, "I guess we can leave your man to the whims of the local police department if you want. Even though you know for a fact they're wrong." She leveled her gaze on Tessa. "I'm good with risking getting my higher-ups a little irritated to do the right thing. But it's your call."

Tessa pursed her lips and didn't even need to think about it. Everyone needed a friend like Gloria. Tessa held out her hand. "Let's go."

With a happy little hop, Gloria grabbed her hand. Tessa expected her to do something to activate the invisibility—wiggle her nose, maybe, or wave a hand. Maybe flap like a chicken. But she didn't do anything. One second, Tessa was looking at Gloria, and the next, she was looking at the tree behind her, unimpeded by her friend's image in front of it.

Tessa glanced down at her own body and gave a little squeak. She'd half-expected to still be able to see herself, but she couldn't.

Disorientation sent her lurching forward when Gloria started to walk, tugging on her hand. Gloria stopped to let Tessa get her footing. "It helps to just keep looking ahead," she whispered. "Don't look down or over at me if you can help it. Your brain will object to the experience."

Object to the experience. Yeah, that's what her brain was doing all right. It made her vision blur and gave her nausea like a bad migraine.

Tessa took a deep breath, looked straight ahead, and started walking slowly.

This is better. I can work with this.

She ignored the remaining slight queasy feeling in her gut and kept moving forward beside Gloria.

They had to skirt around the gate at the end of the driveway which, thankfully, was meant to keep out cars and didn't extend to a fully fenced-in property. They hurried down the driveway, hand in hand.

As the huge house came into view, Tessa could see there were three people, a man and two women, on the porch. A second later, she realized they were arguing.

The invisible reapers jogged forward until they were at the base of the steps, close enough to see and hear what was happening.

"Please don't do this!" The speaker was a woman in her mid to late forties. She wore a white apron and tears streamed down her plump face. "I *need* this job. I love this job. Really, I don't even know what else I could do."

The man, who was bald on top but had a ring of dull-brown hair around the back of his skull and a poufy mustache, crossed his arms. "That really isn't our concern, Lark."

Lark. Was that a name Mrs. Cross had mentioned? No, she'd mentioned another, a woman named Sky who'd taken over as chef when Mrs. Cross moved to the work with the horses. The name was so unusual Tessa remembered it clearly. But she also mentioned that Sky's daughter now worked in her place.

The crying woman had to be her.

Lark cried harder, making all kinds of snorting and huffing noises.

"Nathaniel." The woman, who looked vaguely familiar to Tessa, though she couldn't place her, stepped forward, putting a hand on the man's arm. For a second, Tessa thought she would council the man to let up on Lark but, instead, she addressed the chef. "We're going to call the police either way, but if you want to avoid trespassing charges on top of the other trouble coming your way, you should probably leave our property now."

"But . . ." Lark's eyes shifted between the pair pleadingly.

"What did *my* father say about ifs, ands, or buts?" The woman brushed something off her long, black skirt. She was tall and elegant, with the air of someone used to living comfortably.

"That they're useless in negotiations," Nathaniel said.

Tessa knew Nathaniel's name too. He was Mr. Green's son-in-law. Mrs. Cross hadn't had good things to say about him either.

The two hovered over Lark like vultures.

Then the mansion's front door swung open, and an elderly woman, bent and leaning heavily on a cane, hobbled out. The woman hurried over to give her an arm.

"What's going on?" the older woman croaked, and then her gaze fell on the sobbing Lark. She looked confused, dazed even.

"Mother," the woman at her arm straightened, "we talked about this. Remember? We know for a fact Lark, here, is a murderess. She killed Father."

Lark wailed louder, turning her focus to the elderly woman. "Mrs. Green, I swear I didn't kill your husband. I . . . I loved him. He was always kind to me. And Hannah, you remember when we used to play as girls? I used to come to your holiday parties . . ."

"I remember." Hannah, whom Tessa had realized was Mr. Green's daughter and Nathaniel's wife, looked unsure for a moment. Then she leaned closer to Lark. "I remember it all too well. You were a liar then, and you're just as bold of one now."

"I'm not lying! I don't know why that cleaner was in the kitchen. I made Mr. Green's cereal and served it to him like always. Then I went up to tidy the bedroom." She ended on a sob, putting her face in her hands. "I can't believe he's gone."

Hannah studied the chef. For a second, it looked almost like she did believe her. "Maybe we shouldn't tell the police about this until after Dad's funeral."

"No!" Nathaniel boomed. "She killed him. She needs to be put away."

"But the police arrested someone else. And if we make it public knowledge that Dad was killed by a member of his own staff, won't he look stupid?" Hannah glanced at Lark. "It isn't like she's going to be able to disappear into thin air or anything. We can talk to the police later. After the press loses interest."

Nathaniel was shaking his head almost violently, but Mrs. Green tipped her head. "You may be right, dear. I have no desire to see your father's poor judgement splashed across the newspapers, tarnishing his memory."

"It wouldn't tarnish his memory because I didn't do it. I'll take a lie detector. Whatever it takes."

Hannah set her jaw. "You're not welcome here. Get off our property and don't you *ever* come back."

Lark sobbed even harder, but she didn't argue anymore. She stumbled across the porch and down the stairs.

Tessa and Gloria had to dance out of her way as she hurtled past them.

The three on the porch watched the chef get into a rusty Ford sedan and drive away.

"There," Hannah said. "It's done."

Mrs. Green nodded solemnly. "I need to rest before the funeral director arrives. Will you help me upstairs?"

"Of course, Mom. Let's get you to your chair." Hannah helped the old woman back into the house.

Nathaniel stayed on the porch, staring up the driveway where Lark had disappeared. He frowned.

Gloria tugged on Tessa's arm, and they headed away from the house too.

Tessa let her mind wander while Gloria led the way.

It made sense that the chef would have great access to Mr. Green's food. But why would she poison him if she depended so much on the job? It seemed like she wasn't well-liked by anyone else in the family and the old man had been the only reason Lark stayed employed there.

Still, it was more likely to have been the chef than Silas. At least Tessa had somewhere to start her investigation.

Chapter 9

"Well, here we are. Back where we began." Gloria put the car in park. They'd spent the rest of the day on three additional reaps, with Gloria giving Tessa tips now and then.

Tessa hadn't needed to use her special badge—the reaps had all been in private homes or outside where no one else was around. She'd made a mental note to figure out a good spot to keep the lanyard when she wasn't working. She could easily imagine herself losing the thing and then having to frantically search everywhere for it.

She hopped out of Gloria's car and then stuck her head back through the doorway. "Thanks for everything today. You're a great boss!"

Gloria chuckled and made a shooing motion. "Go on. I'm having dinner with Ella, and I don't want to be late."

"Have fun. Hey, ask her about that Thai food, will ya?"

Gloria drove off in a hurry. Good thing Linda fired right up with no problem. But before Tessa could put the car into reverse, already thinking about Silas and what she may be able to do next for him, her phone buzzed. She pulled it out to see a text from her mom: *Care to come over for dinner at seven?*

Tessa chewed her bottom lip for a second, wondering what to do. Once again, it was late in the evening, and Tessa had no idea how she could possibly help Silas. Gloria had put her investigation in the right direction. But it wasn't like she was a detective. She was a reaper. And her mother was now even higher up in the pecking order. Maybe she could offer some insight that neither Tessa nor Gloria had thought of yet.

Tessa's stomach grumbled, clinching the decision. She typed back quickly: *Sure. Need me to bring anything?*

The answer came almost immediately: *I think I'm all set.*

It was just like Cheryl to be "all set." She was Type A in every single way, which included hosting others for dinner—even her own daughter. She'd been that way as long as Tessa could remember.

Tessa wondered how her mother had managed it all. Cheryl kept the house clean, got dinner prepped and ready by seven every night, and still maintained a solid relationship with Tessa's father. And she did that between reaps, PTA, choir practice, and attending Tessa's extracurricular activities.

The clock on Linda's dashboard said it was before six o'clock. Tessa considered going to her apartment for a little while but quickly decided against it. Maybe she could learn a few other things from her mother. She drove straight to her mom's house and parked on the street out front.

As usual, pulling up to her childhood home brought on a flood of memories and emotions. She'd had a good childhood, if a tiny bit lonely as an only child. So, most of the memories were good. Still, Tessa always thought about her dad as she walked the familiar path up the driveway to the front door. She really missed him, and whenever something new happened in her life, she always wondered how he would react to it.

Her mind drifted to Silas, and she imagined bringing him home to meet her dad. She had no doubt they'd get along, since both men liked working with their hands and putting in an honest day's labor.

It was more than that, though. Silas was the first guy she'd ever thought this way about. Her heart squeezed at the thought that the two men would never get to sit down and have a meal together or commiserate over Tessa's less desirable traits.

She entered the house and called out, so she wouldn't startle her mom.

Cheryl appeared in the kitchen doorway wearing an apron. "You're an hour early, Theresa. Dinner's not ready." Her tone of voice seemed to indicate that Tessa should turn around and leave the house.

Tessa shook her head. "Sorry. I just had nothing to do for an hour, so I decided to come on over. Maybe I could help you with dinner?"

Cheryl's face twisted for a second in an expression that clearly showed she had doubts about Tessa's ability to help. She quickly smoothed the wrinkles in her forehead out. "You? Help with dinner?"

Tessa rolled her eyes. "Come on, Mom. I *can* cook a little bit. Besides, I could use a lesson or two. You can teach me more, so I'll get better at it."

"I tried to when you were in high school."

"I wasn't ready for it then." *No, I was dealing with other stuff.* She batted her eyelashes a little bit and tried to look younger.

Cheryl sighed and headed back into the kitchen. "Come on, then."

Tessa dropped her purse on a chair in the living room on her way through to the kitchen. "Smells good in here. What are we having?"

"Roasted chicken and vegetables. You can chop the potatoes." Cheryl gestured toward a bowl full of russets on the counter. "I already scrubbed them."

Tessa washed her hands in the kitchen sink and then began chopping. Cheryl was busy seasoning the bird, which was already in a roasting pan.

"So, how was your first day as the Eastern district supervisor?" Tessa asked.

"Horrible. There was a mound of paperwork and video conferencing—between which I had plenty of additional regulations to read." She cut her eyes toward Tessa. "You know, all the job description type of stuff that you skimmed over when you started *your* new job."

With a smirk, Tessa dropped a handful of newly chopped potatoes into the pan. "I figured you'd tell me anything truly important."

"Yes, well, my boss isn't so accommodating as yours was."

Tessa thought about Corwin Blade. He'd been pretty nice to her, but she could imagine it wouldn't be good to be on his bad side. As a grim reaper, getting fired isn't the worst thing that could happen when important rules get broken. At least, that's what Cheryl had hinted at now and then.

"The secret is to stuff bits of butter and herbs under the skin." Cheryl demonstrated, showing Tessa how to season the chicken. "The second secret is to not overcook it."

"But it's chicken." Tessa eyed it as if just looking at it might give her salmonella.

"A lot of people are antsy about chicken, and they want to make extra sure it's done. So, I have a secret weapon to guard against that." Cheryl held up a meat thermometer.

"That's it? Not very glamorous. I thought you were going to show me a *real* secret," Tessa teased. "Like one from the big guy." She cut her eyes toward her mother. "You have one of those, don't you?"

Cheryl gave no indication she knew what Tessa was talking about. "I have a thermometer, dear. I pull the chicken out of the oven when it's about five degrees below where I want it to end up. It'll continue to cook a bit and finish up once it's out. That's another thing a lot of people don't realize about chicken. If you cook it until it gets to the temperature you're going for before taking it out, it will be overcooked."

Tessa dumped the rest of the potato chunks into the roasting pan, and Cheryl slid the whole thing into the oven. Then she turned toward her daughter, and her eyes dropped to Tessa's chest. "What's that?"

Tessa's hand flew up. Did her V-neck dip too low? But when her fingertips brushed the special badge, she winced internally. She'd gotten distracted with memories when she arrived at Cheryl's house and hadn't taken it off.

"A reaper badge," Tessa said cautiously, unsure whether her mother was upset or not. "Gloria said you didn't think I was ready for this, but she does."

Cheryl's expression wasn't readable. "She's your direct supervisor now. I won't have time to micromanage all of the agency managers, nor do I care to. If Gloria's wrong, she'll have to deal with the consequences."

Not exactly a ringing endorsement of either Gloria's managerial skills or Tessa's ability to not screw up her new responsibilities. But in the world of Cheryl Randolph, it was pretty good. Tessa decided to take it as a victory and not push her luck.

Cheryl crossed the room and pulled two wine glasses out of the antique hutch there. She splashed what Tessa guessed was close to an exact ounce of red wine into each of them and handed her daughter one. "Care to sit on the back porch while the chicken roasts?" She grinned. "Since you were early."

Tessa accepted the glass and followed her mother through the house and out the back door. Cheryl glanced over her shoulder. "Do you need a sweater? The evening's a bit chilly."

"I think I'll be okay."

They settled into chairs and sipped in silence for a few minutes, each looking over the back yard and its prim landscaping.

Finally, Cheryl said, "So, did you have a chance to use that today?" She tipped her head toward the badge.

"Gloria mentored me on several reaps. I used the badge at the hospital for an elderly woman and again at the chemical plant. But I didn't need it for the rest of them." She wasn't about to tell her mom they'd gone to Mr. Green's property and used Gloria's new invisibility to spy on the people there. Cheryl was in a more flexible, sweet mood than usual, but there was no way she'd condone what they'd done, even if it was to help an innocent man escape wrongful charges.

As though Cheryl picked Silas out of Tessa's thoughts, she said, "I heard about your landlord being arrested for Artemis Green's murder."

Maybe it was the wine. More likely, it was being in her childhood home and all the feelings that brought up. But whatever it was, Tessa felt herself sort of crumble inside at her mother's words. "It was all my fault. Gloria was right. I shouldn't have lied to him. If I hadn't, he never would have followed me on Mr. Green's reap and gotten himself caught on camera." The words sounded anguished, even to her own ears, but she couldn't help it.

Still, as soon as they were out of her mouth, Tessa regretted saying them. She just knew Cheryl would give her a dressing down for putting Silas in harm's way.

Only she didn't. She did something else entirely.

Cheryl smiled slightly, mostly in her eyes. "You really like him, don't you?"

Tessa had to fight through her startled feelings to choke out an answer. "He's a really nice guy."

"Cute too." Cheryl winked.

Tessa's laughter surprised her. "Mom!" she chided. But then she shrugged and admitted, "Super cute."

"I know I'm not your supervisor anymore, so maybe my opinion on this doesn't matter, but I don't agree with Gloria. I don't think this is your fault—you weren't lying to Silas just for the sake of lying. You were trying to protect him. You didn't know it would work out this way." She gazed across the back yard, a wistful look on her face. "We so often can't predict what our loved ones will do."

Tessa knew Cheryl was remembering Michael Randolph, who had made a decision to take Tessa's place when she was scheduled to die. Cheryl hadn't known her husband was going to do it.

As though dragging herself back to the current time, Cheryl returned her gaze to her daughter. "Things will work out for your Silas. The police still have a lot of work to do to prove he's guilty of Mr. Green's murder."

They fell into silence again, sipping wine and losing themselves in their own thoughts. Tessa wasn't so sure that the police would do much more to prove Silas's guilt. The words that Mrs. Cross had used, *open and shut case*, drifted back to her.

But thinking about her elderly neighbor gave Tessa an idea about where to go next in her own investigation.

Chapter 10

Tessa sort of thought it wasn't a regular thing for grim reapers to have a day off. At least, when she'd looked over her contract, that wasn't included.

Oh, she had plenty of time off—when she wasn't actively on a reap or filling out paperwork, Tessa could pretty much do whatever she wanted. But, still, unless she specifically requested vacation time and her jobs were shifted to other reapers in the agency, Tessa expected to work some every day.

How did that idiom go? There were two certainties in life and the death one kept her and many other reapers busy. She wondered if taxes were so certain, how come accountants only worked hard one or two months of the year?

But when she got up the morning after having dinner with Cheryl, her app was blank. There were no reaps scheduled for her that day.

"Thanks, Gloria." Tessa smiled. Clearly, her friend had arranged it so Tessa would have the day free to investigate Artemis Green's murder. And luckily, she knew exactly where she wanted to begin.

She gathered her supplies, making sure to grab the magical badge Gloria had given her the day before, and headed out the door.

Her intention was to knock on Mrs. Cross's door and see if she knew Lark's address. But Tessa was surprised to find Mrs. Cross already in the hallway, heading for the lobby. The bandana was no longer on her head, and the curlers were out, tight round tunnels of hair left in their wake.

"Good morning, Mrs. Cross!" Tessa hurried to catch up with the elderly lady. "Where are you off to so early?"

The elderly woman glared at Tessa, who held her breath, figuring the woman was going to tell her off and refuse to help.

Instead, Mrs. Cross puffed out a breath. "Well, I wouldn't normally consider it to be any of your business, girl. But, since it's to do with that dreadful murder your boyfriend committed, I'll tell you."

Tessa ground her teeth, thinking better than to respond. She needed Mrs. Cross's help.

"I'm going to visit Sky. She called me last night, distraught. Now, she and I don't normally have a lot of love lost between us, you know. But those idiot relatives of Artemis's fired her daughter Lark, who takes care of her now. I thought I'd go over and check in on them. See how they're doing."

"What did they fire her for?" Tessa hoped she looked and sounded appropriately clueless and not at all like someone who had used invisibility magic to listen in on the mentioned firing.

"Bah." Mrs. Cross looked so disgusted Tessa thought she might spit on the hallway carpet. "Apparently, Nathaniel's accusing her of killing Artemis."

Tessa felt like there was an opportunity here, but she had to think fast. She started speaking slowly and picked up steam as the idea coalesced. "Um, you know, if Lark thinks she was wrongfully terminated, the law office I work for may be interested in hearing about the case."

Mrs. Cross leaned more heavily on her cane and peered at Tessa, who tried to keep her face from revealing the lie. "You work for a lawyer?" The wrinkles on her forehead were even deeper than usual.

"That's right. I'm a paralegal." Tessa swallowed hard, steeled herself, and lifted the badge, hoping fervently that it would show appropriate credentials for a paralegal. Would the magic work if Tessa wasn't using it for an actual reap? And if she was lying for personal gain?

She reminded herself it wasn't personal. Tessa was trying to right a wrong here. Silas definitely hadn't killed Mr. Green. All she was trying to do was prove that by revealing who had. Surely, the universe or Grim Reaper magic or whatever it was that was responsible for making the badge work would be interested in aiding that honorable intent.

And just to add some extra oomph, she crossed her fingers behind her back. It never hurt to hedge your bets.

Mrs. Cross squinted at the badge. She adjusted her glasses and squinted harder. Tessa held it out farther, until her neighbor's nose was about an inch from the picture.

Silence fell over the hallway, except for the sound of someone's television blaring a morning talk show from inside a nearby apartment.

The woman's forehead scrunched and her nose wrinkled, pulling her upper lip off her teeth and making her resemble a beaver.

Finally, she backed away from the badge. Tessa waited for her to announce it was blank. But, instead, she said, "Well, then. If that's the case, you may as well come with me to see them. You can drive."

A flood of relief made Tessa feel like giggling. She bit it back and opened the door to the lobby to let Mrs. Cross through. As they passed the front desk, Tessa felt a stab of melancholy at the fact that it was empty. Silas would probably be absolutely buried in work when he returned. He always had a long to-do list, and missing work would leave him behind.

Maybe she could get Gloria to give her another day off to help him catch up when he got released.

If he got released.

Mrs. Cross complained about one thing or another the entire trip to Lark's place. First, about Tessa's driving. She was going too fast, then too slow. Finally, her complaints broadened outside the car. The hairdresser hadn't been able to get her in when she wanted. The thermostat in her apartment made the place colder when she wanted it warmer. That murderous landlord had probably set the chemicals wrong in the pool and that's why she had eczema on her ankles during the summer.

Tessa was grateful when Mrs. Cross pointed to their left, almost bashing Tessa in the nose with her arm, and barked, "There! Pull in."

It was a more modest apartment building, even, than Mist River Manor, which would never be called lavish in any circle. The sign out front said King's Court. At least, that's what Tessa thought it said. Several letters on the painted sign were faded and peeled enough to be unrecognizable.

She ran around to open the passenger side and offered Mrs. Cross her arm, which the elderly woman took to haul herself out of Linda. Tessa reached past her to grab the cane.

"Which apartment?" she wondered as they approached the run-down building, which looked more like a motel than apartments, with a line of doors that all opened to the outside.

"That one." Mrs. Cross pointed with a trembling finger at one of the doors.

Lark answered after only one knock. "Oh, hello, Louise." She didn't smile when she addressed Mrs. Cross. Then her eyes swept to Tessa. "Who's this?"

"My neighbor." Mrs. Cross started to walk forward, forcing Lark to step aside or risk bruised toes. "She works for a lawyer, so I brought her to see if there's anything to be done for your situation."

Tessa hesitated, hoping Lark would formally invite her over the threshold, but the chef only thinned her lips and stared, so she tiptoed in after Mrs. Cross.

The apartment was neat and clean, though sparsely appointed. They were in a tiny living room, where Mrs. Cross already sat in a sky-blue armchair and a loveseat was the only other seat. An old-style tube TV sat on a worn wooden table and a crossword puzzle book lay open on a chipped up white painted coffee table.

"I guess you'd better have a seat. Do you want any tea or water?" Lark's tone revealed she was a reluctant hostess.

"No, thank you," Tessa answered. "We won't take much of your time. Mrs. Cross told me you were wrongfully terminated from your position on Artemis Green's staff, and I wondered if my firm may be able to help."

She shrugged, misery etched on her features. "I doubt it. Nathaniel is ruling the roost now, and he's a worm. I doubt your lawyers will be nearly as venomous as his."

"Lark! Where are your manners? You shouldn't talk ill of others in mixed company." A barefoot woman dressed in a turquoise and cream peasant skirt and cream linen top with sleeves that ended in wide, flowing openings, entered the living room from a hallway. She had buttery blonde hair swept up in a loose bun at the nape of her neck. She smiled brightly at Tessa and then Mrs. Cross, though it faltered at the edges on her.

"What mixed company, Ma?" Lark looked baffled. "It's Louise Cross who used to work at the Green place with you and a paralegal lady."

Lark's mother crossed the room in a sashay that, combined with the peasant skirt, made her appear to be floating. She shook Mrs. Cross's hand and then Tessa's. "I'm Sky. Welcome to our home." She waved a hand around and a frown tugged at her lips. "Such as it is."

With a groan, Lark threw herself into the love seat next to Tessa. "You know how I feel about that, Ma," she grumbled.

Sky ignored her daughter and perched on the edge of the coffee table, since there weren't any more real chairs. Tessa figured she was around Mr. and Mrs. Green's age, but she looked healthy, like Artemis had, rather than frail like Mrs. Green—or Mrs. Cross.

Sky blew out a puff of breath. "Yes, I know how you feel about it, dear. And we did it your way, didn't we? That's why we'll be stuck in this apartment forever."

"To be fair," Lark leveled her gaze on her mother, "we live this way because of the way I was raised. Can I help it if I took some notes from my mother?"

"A woman can change her mind," Sky said. "I thought it was best at the time. Now, we'll only be here for as long as the money lasts. Then, we'll have to find a new place to live."

"I'll find another job." Lark sounded exhausted, as though they'd had this conversation many times recently. "I'm sure I can find something at a local restaurant or hotel or something. I can cook and clean."

Sky waved a hand. "Yes, yes." Her tone was resigned. "We'll make do, I suppose." She glanced at Tessa and Mrs. Cross as though she'd forgotten the other two women were in her living room. "Recently, we had a chance to do better, you know. Now, that's gone forever."

"Because Lark was fired?" Tessa guessed. "I was actually hoping to hear about that."

But Sky was already shaking her head. "No, no. She was never going to get rich working for Artemis. But she gave up her chance of getting the real money that was due to her."

"What was due to you?" Tessa was confused.

Sky sent a look of question over to Lark, who nodded as if allowing her mother to say whatever she was about to reveal.

"Lark is his. We had an affair about a year or so after I began working for him. You see, his wife wasn't doing well at the time, and he just needed some companionship. Honestly, it was a fling. I was a free spirit at the time. And it wasn't like it is today. I couldn't be sure that she was his.

"Still, he offered me a huge amount of money for us to just go away—disappear into the night."

"And you didn't take it." Lark shook her head, smiling lovingly at her mother.

"I was silly. Money didn't mean a thing to me, and I thought you needed your father in your life. Working there, I was able to bring her along many days. Artemis practically treated her like one of his own while they were together."

"You did the right thing, Ma. I loved getting to know him. My half-sister too, even if I couldn't tell her we were related. And you were right—money isn't the answer to anyone's prayers. Just look at what it's done to Hannah and Nathaniel."

Sky glanced at her daughter. "Of course, now I'm regretting the way I raised you."

"Why do you say that?" Tessa asked.

"Because she refused him again! About a month ago, he offered to give Lark her inheritance but on the condition that she quit her job. And she refused! Refused the huge sum that he tried to give her. Instead, she begged to be allowed to stay on, so she could be near him every day."

"There are things in life that are more important than money, Ma." Lark's tone was firm.

Tessa's mind raced, trying to catch up with the story Sky had told. But her mind was stuck on the first point. "So, Artemis Green was your father?"

These words startled Mrs. Cross out of some sort of stupor. "What was that? I still had my cheaters tuned to the radio."

"I was just telling your friend that Lark is Mr. Green's daughter."

Lark nodded, and Tessa said, "And why couldn't you tell Hannah?"

"I couldn't tell anybody. My father was afraid it would upset his wife so much that she may have a stroke or heart attack or something. She's been frail since her sickness." Lark shrugged. "Plus, the whole affair thing. I went along with it to make my dad happy. And it was worth it. I got to be near him. Talk to him. He was very kind to me. It was a win-win situation. Until now."

Sky spoke up. "Yes, now, everything is over. You don't have your father anymore, and you don't have any of the money you're due because you're his daughter just as much as Hannah is. I'd say I told you so, but that ship has sailed."

"It isn't really Hannah who's going to inherit the money anyway," Lark snapped. When her mother opened her mouth to argue, Lark held up a hand. "Nathaniel works at my father's company. Hannah's a mouse. Her husband controls her and everything about their marriage. He's really the one who's going to control the inheritance. I'm sure he'll run my dad's property *and* his business into the ground. Perhaps my dear sister and I will meet again in the poorhouse."

Mrs. Cross clucked her tongue. "You should've taken the money and run, girl. Who turns down a fortune just to hang out with an old man and wait on his family hand and foot?"

Lark glared at Mrs. Cross. "I know this may be news to you, Louise, but, like I said before, there are more important things in life than money."

Mrs. Cross scoffed. "A little money never hurt anyone."

Tessa withheld a giggle. She knew through Silas that Mrs. Cross played the lottery every week.

Lark sighed. "No, but a lot of money can. I saw that close-up living in the Green household. Nathaniel has been completely spoiled by having wealth he didn't earn himself. He's a wretched man now. I'm glad I didn't take the money and become like that myself. In fact, that money made him *murderous*." She snarled the last word.

"You think Nathaniel killed Mr. Green?" Tessa guessed.

"Of course, he did. Who else would have? And why else would he be the one trying to get rid of me so quicky? I know they arrested some other poor slob for it, and they're trying to push me into being a secondary fall guy if the first one doesn't hold. But I know beyond a shadow of a doubt that Nathaniel's the one who poisoned my dad and tried to frame me for it."

Sky reached out and took her daughter's hand. "It's going to be okay."

"No, Ma, it's not." She let her head fall back against the loveseat and murmured, "The sad part is I think he'll probably get away with it."

Chapter 11

Again, it felt like Gloria was going easy on her. Tessa only had one reap that morning and the rest of the day was hers to do as she pleased. Normally, that meant streaming a few rom-coms after eating lunch out at her favorite dive restaurant. Tessa saw no comedies in her future. But there was always time for a burger and fries.

She stared across the street. It helped that her favorite greasy spoon was situated just across the road from Artemis Green's company, aptly named Green Holdings and Properties.

She thought about barging inside, using her badge to gain entrance. The only problem with that was she didn't have a solid plan for what to do or how to deal with anything she found once she got inside. She racked her brain for a plan while she dipped hand-cut fries into a mound of ketchup.

Sheila's Diner served burgers so greasy they'd disintegrate the paper if you tried to take them to go. A thick milkshake helped to wash the gut bomb down.

Tessa paid and gathered up her things. She decided to just do it—just walk across the street and go in. She resolved to hope for some good fortune to come her way, however unlikely. Then, good fortune slipped right past her in the diner's doorway, wearing way too much cologne.

Nathaniel shoved his way inside, never minding that Tessa was already midway through the exit. She gasped as his elbow shoved her in the side and then turned to watch him tip his head toward the cashier and pick up a brown paper bag, already laden with grease on the bottom.

Big mistake.

In only a few seconds, he'd brushed past Tessa again and hopped into a Mercedes illegally parked in a handicap spot out front.

Finally, her brain clicked on. Tessa went into high gear, rushing to Linda and not giving the old gal a choice but to roar to life. She revved the engine, then sped off in pursuit of the much fancier car.

She was focused on the road, making turn after turn but trying not to tail Nathaniel too closely, when her phone rang with an unknown number.

Tessa was used to calls from debt collectors from before—when she'd worked as a waitress at Frank's restaurant and lived paycheck to paycheck. But it'd been months since becoming a reaper had landed her squarely in financially stable territory. She'd paid off everything.

"I don't owe you anything," she answered, flipping the phone to speaker mode.

On the other end of the line, a robotic voice said, "Will you accept a collect call from Silas St. Onge?"

"Silas? Uh, yeah. Sure."

There was a moment's pause before the lines clicked over and she heard Silas's breathing, slow and steady, into the receiver. "Silas?"

"Tessa, hey."

"Hi." She didn't really know what to say. She wondered why he'd choose to call her. Didn't he only get one phone call? And he had to be so mad. Plus, she was a little busy. Linda was having trouble keeping up with the more performant vehicle, and Tessa had no clue where Nathaniel was heading. It wasn't to Mr. Green's mansion.

In fact, they were pointed toward the opposite side of town. *Maybe the casino?* She hadn't been that way in a long time, not since chasing down Chet Sanborn's spirit.

"Are you busy?" Silas asked.

"Kind of," she admitted.

"Okay, well, this won't take long. I don't really have a lot of time."

"Silas, shouldn't you be calling your lawyer or something?"

He laughed, full-throated and genial. She hadn't thought she'd hear his laugh ever again, not like that. "That's not exactly how it works. I've already talked—I've already *seen* my lawyer a bunch. And I do get a few minutes for personal calls."

"Oh."

"That's all you have to say, considering the circumstance I'm in?"

"No." She bit her lip, making another turn. "I've got a lot to say. For one, I'm sorry. I'm really, *really* sorry."

"I know you are. And look, it's partially my fault."

"Okay?"

"Yeah. I'll just get to the point." He sighed. "I know. I know how you act in situations like this. And I wanted to tell you not to."

"Not to what?"

"Not to do whatever it is you're doing right now. You're trying to get me out, aren't you?"

"Well, sort of . . ."

"Just don't. Okay? That's why I called. I want you to sit this one out."

"Oh, you've got to be kidding me!" Tessa groaned.

"What? What's up?"

Tessa couldn't tell Silas the real reason she'd blurted out those words—because they'd undermine her cause. He'd just asked her to do the opposite of what she was doing. She couldn't exactly tell him that Nathaniel had pulled into her old nemesis, the Sweetwater Golf Course.

"I can't just let you rot in prison." Tessa pulled into a spot toward the back of the lot.

"I'm not in prison. It's jail. And yes, you can. I've got a lawyer. The police can find the *real* killer."

"They won't," Tessa argued.

"You can't know that. I've got to go. Please, just listen to me for once. I'm fine. I don't need your help." He hung up before she could get another word in edgewise.

*　*　*

Nathaniel went inside the clubhouse and came back to his car with a golf cart. He loaded it with a set of clubs from his trunk, then set the brown paper bag, which was getting soggier by the minute, on the seat next to him.

Seriously?

Lark and Mrs. Cross hadn't been wrong about Nathaniel. There were so many other things he could be doing right now in the middle of the day. He could be working. He could be comforting his wife, who'd just lost her father. Instead, he was spending his father-in-law's money to play a round of golf.

Tessa seethed, not only at Nathaniel but also at the golf course. It was the scene of her very first reap and also where she'd had to perform some reaper trickeration to send Chet Sanborn's killer to the white lights that greeted everyone when their time came to an end. She hated this and every other golf course. It was like some sort of cosmic joke that she ended up on one so often.

Tessa did some quick thinking. *What would Gloria do in this situation?* Gloria would have the perfect outfit in the trunk of her car. Tessa wasn't so lucky. But she did have a paid-off credit card. She went in the clubhouse, found a pastel polo, a skirt, and some golf shoes, then bought a half dozen drinks from the cooler.

The cashier asked if she'd like to pay for a round of golf, but when she saw the price, her eyes bulged. It was the same as she'd pay for the outfit and drinks! She lied and told him that her husband would be there shortly, finding a random name on the tee times list somewhere below Nathaniel Neilson.

"Ah! Very good, then," the cashier said.

Tessa smiled and hoped he wouldn't notice when she stole a golf cart to chase Nathaniel down on the first tee.

She changed in the lady's locker room, then made her way to the practice green where a line of golf carts sat with the keys inside. Stealing a golf cart had to be the easiest thing she'd done all week.

But Nathaniel wasn't on the first hole. He wasn't on the second tee either. He played fast. She found him at the turn before the third tee, sitting in his golf cart and enjoying the greasy burger from Sheila's.

"Need something to wash that down?" She pulled alongside him.

Momentarily, he was taken aback. "Do you work here?"

She nodded. "I'm the new cart girl." She hoped she remembered the lingo. Hadn't her first reap thought that's who she had to be?

"Oh." Nathaniel scowled. "I thought you folks had a special cart."

Tessa wanted to slap her forehead. Of course the cart girl had a special cart to carry the snacks and beverages. Here she was with a regular cart and six cans of various soda. "It's, uh, it's in the shop. We had to make do with this. You want anything or not?" A little attitude always helped in situations like this.

"Uh, sure." He nodded, still skeptical, but dug in his back pocket for his wallet. He handed her a twenty, picked a diet soda, and told her to keep the change.

Twenty dollars for a soda. *Yeah, he really doesn't know anything about money.*

His face told her she'd already worn out her welcome. Tessa gave the cart a little gas but stopped abruptly. "Hey! Wait." Her tone made a one-eighty from before. "You're Nathaniel Neilson, right?"

"You . . . you know who I am?"

"Of course I do!" she said. "You're practically as famous as your father-in law. You work at Green Holdings, right? I was so sad to hear about Mr. Green's passing."

"It's a tragedy," Nathaniel said mournfully.

"Does that mean you're running things there now?"

"I, um. Yes, I guess it does." He glanced around the greenery, maybe a tad embarrassed he wasn't there working now. "It basically runs itself these days, though."

"I'm sure." Tessa nodded encouragingly. "I'm just glad they caught the guy who did it. I'm sure you are too."

Nathaniel winced. "I'm afraid I don't think they've got the right person."

"No?" Tessa wondered if he was truly being honest. Did he really think Lark was the culprit? Maybe so. But Tessa wasn't convinced.

"It's a very complicated family dynamic. I'm sure you understand."

"Not really," Tessa replied.

"I'm sure you have other golfers to attend to. "This time, it was crystal clear he was meaning to shoo her away. He stretched and rubbed at his back. "And, you know what? I think I pulled a muscle in the last sand trap. I'd better be heading back. It was nice meeting you."

He nodded, threw his cart in reverse, and looped around her, heading back in the direction of the club house.

Now, Tessa was sure he was lying. Only she didn't know about what.

Chapter 12

Exhausted wasn't the right word to describe how Tessa felt as she fell into bed. She squirmed into her favorite position, on her right side with her knees drawn up a bit. With a deep sigh, she stared into the darkness and began to count slowly from fifty back toward zero. Somewhere around thirty-nine, her eyelids began to get heavy and slide shut.

A horrifying noise from the inky black corner of the room stabbed through the silence and caused Tessa to roll out of bed and onto her feet in a crouch, as though she may need to defend herself. But the fast movement made her dizzy, and she wobbled and then crashed back against the bed.

No matter what Silas thought, she was never going to be a superhero. If anything, he was the superhero around the apartment complex. And with him gone, there were already grumblings about broken furnaces and the leaves piling up around the pool.

But there hadn't been any sort of talk about break-ins. Tessa scoured her room for a pointy or heavy club-like object. Either or would do, but both was preferred.

The sound repeated, and Tessa recognized it this time. She called off the internal search for a weapon.

"Pepper!" She groaned as she managed to get her feet under her and flipped on the bedside lamp. Sure enough, the cat was in the corner, sitting next to a giant hair ball, looking proud of herself.

"Are *you* going to clean it up?" Tessa put her hands on her hips and stared at the tortie cat, who stared back impassively, eyes half-lidded.

After a moment, Pepper stalked away from the mess, hopped up onto Tessa's bed, and curled into a tight ball. She closed her eyes, giving a clear signal to Tessa that it was her job to clean up.

"Fine. But don't ask me for any canned food for the next week," Tessa grumbled.

After she'd taken care of the mess, Tessa climbed back into bed, making sure to snap the blankets in such a way that it would disturb Pepper. The cat lifted her head and gave Tessa a searing glare.

"Hey, I'm just returning the favor." Tessa grinned and then settled herself back into her favorite position, snapping off the bedside lamp. She closed her eyes and started at fifty again, slowly counting backward.

This time, the horrible sound that erupted into the black night definitely wasn't the cat bringing up a hairball.

In fact, Pepper was just as startled by the harsh, blaring siren noise. Eyes wide with feral panic, the cat leaped off the bed and ran out of the room, her claws making a scratching noise as they dug into the carpet to give her more momentum.

Tessa sat up, flipped on the lamp again, and reached for her phone—the thing making the horrible klaxon sound. She looked at the screen and noticed it was the reaper app trying to get her attention. She'd never heard it make a sound like that before.

Never a dull moment with this job.

She frantically swept at the screen, trying to get it to shut off. The apartment's walls weren't particularly thick, and she could already imagine the neighbors pounding on her door to yell at her.

After fifteen seconds of frantically pawing at the device, Tessa was able to get the alarm off and open the reaper app to discover the thing had been making such a horrid noise because there was a reap happening in less than fifteen minutes.

Tessa leaped out of bed, thinking that she must've missed the original notification. She scrolled through the assignment, scanning the text to find out where she was supposed to show up, but her eyes focused on the name of the assignment instead. Her heart pounded in her ears—she recognized that name. She more than recognized that name.

The time of death and the estimated time of arrival—both provided by the app—were very close. Too close. Tessa glanced down at herself. She was in pajama pants and a long-sleeved shirt, so she decided to call it good enough.

Clutching her phone in her hand, she rushed out of her room, through the apartment, and out the door. She was several steps down the hallway before she skidded to a stop, did an about-face, and rushed back into the apartment to slip on a pair of flip-flops. She knew her feet would probably freeze and turn blue in the cool night, but she didn't have time for anything else. The assignment's address was at least ten minutes from the apartment building, if she ignored the speed limit. There was almost no way she could make it in time.

Thankfully, Linda started right up. In fact, she seemed raring to go, which was good, because by the time Tessa was on the road, she only had seven minutes to get to the reap. It was in the same general neighborhood as Artemis Green's house, which was also lucky because Tessa had been there several times in recent days, so she was confident of the route.

This place didn't have a gate out front, and it wasn't as majestic of a home as Mr. Greens, but in Tessa's world, it still qualified as a mansion. It was white clapboard colonial style, and there was one other car in the driveway. Tessa jumped out of Linda and hastily checked the upper corners of the porch for cameras, but, unlike at the Green residence, didn't spot any.

She crept up to the front door, half expecting guard dogs or something to leap out of the darkness at her. But nothing happened, and the doorknob turned easily under her hand. She eased herself through the doorway into a big, marble-floored lobby with a spiral staircase in the center. The area was dimly lit by the soft light of a single lamp on the far side of the room.

Movement to her left caught Tessa's attention, and she swung around, trying to think of a way to explain her presence in the home if she got caught by a family or staff member.

But it wasn't her assignment or a member of his household coming out of the doorway. Tessa recognized Jake, another reaper in her office. His expression was grim, which wasn't like him.

Any other time Tessa had ever interacted with Jake, he'd been jovial and friendly—a jokester who liked to have fun. But now, he looked positively solemn. The lamplight cast shadows on his face, which added to the somber effect. He stopped short when he saw her. "Oh, hey."

Tessa glanced over his shoulder into the dark room behind him. "What's going on? I got some weird alarm on the reaper app that I'd never seen before."

"Oh, it was an emergency reap. Something that wasn't on the schedule until the last minute. Everyone within a certain proximity gets a notification, and we're all supposed to rush there in hopes that someone makes it in time. I was able to get here first."

Tessa was moving forward before she consciously decided to, scooting past Jake into a well-appointed office that made the words *man cave* leap into Tessa's mind. Everything was all leather and mahogany. But it was lacking in books. There was a stale smell of cigar smoke, but it wasn't foul smelling. If anything, it was the opposite.

Nathaniel, Artemis Green's son-in-law, sat slumped in a fine leather chair behind a huge, glisteningly clean desk. Tessa could've almost believed he was sleeping if it weren't for the extreme slackness in his facial muscles and the open pill bottle next to a half-full glass of water on the desk in front of him.

Tessa moved farther into the room to look at the pills without touching the bottle. She couldn't read the label in the dim lighting, but she could read the big words scrawled on the note that sat next to it:

I'm sorry. I made a huge mistake when I killed my father-in-law. I couldn't live with it. Please forgive me.

Tessa turned to Jake, who had reentered the room with her. "What did he say? His soul, I mean, when you took it over?"

Jake grimaced and ran a hand through dull-copper-colored hair. "I don't usually ask them questions. I've found I sleep better at night when I don't. But he did seem a little confused. Lots of rapid blinking and looking around."

"Confused? If he killed himself, why would he be confused?"

"Well, it happens sometimes when people don't believe in an afterlife. They're surprised to find that they still have a form of consciousness after their death. It seems to happen a lot with suicides."

Tessa pressed her lips together and looked around the room, but there weren't any other obvious clues. "You sure that's what happened? He committed suicide?"

Jake shrugged. "I guess I can't be sure. By the time I got here, he was already dead. Luckily, his soul was just standing there, like I said, confused."

With a start, Tessa realized they were talking in normal voices. What if they got caught? She lowered her volume. "Have you seen anyone else here?"

He shook his head. "I don't think anybody's home. Listen, I'm going to take off. I want to get a little bit of shuteye tonight before work. You know how it goes with our job—never a day off." He gave her a wry smile.

Tessa nodded. "Have a good night. I'll be right behind you."

But when Jake left the house, Tessa didn't immediately follow. Instead, she made her way quickly through all the rooms on the ground floor. All empty. Next, she crept up the spiral staircase in the center of the foyer and did a quick check of all the rooms up there. They were equally dark and deserted, including what was obviously the master bedroom.

Where was Hannah? It was the middle of the night—shouldn't she be sleeping in her own bed?

Tessa went back to the office and looked one more time over the note. Nathaniel's penmanship was exquisite. He'd even signed his name—probably something he was used to doing working at Mr. Green's business.

Beside the note, there was an open envelope and a letter addressed to Nathaniel and Hannah. It was from Mr. Green's estate attorney about his will. They were going to have a meeting at the residence.

A bit unorthodox.

But even more interesting, Tessa found Lark's name amongst those invited to attend. Maybe Sky was wrong. Maybe Lark was going to come into some money after all.

She hoped so.

Tessa made one last look around, satisfied that she was truly there alone. Then she hurriedly retreated, making her way back out to Linda.

It seemed like an open and shut case, like Mrs. Cross had called Artemis Green's murder. Nathaniel, feeling guilty about having killed Mr. Green, had taken an overdose of pills. It made complete sense.

So why was Tessa's gut telling her that Nathaniel's death hadn't been a suicide?

Chapter 13

Tessa made her way through the lobby of Mist River Manor Apartments with her thoughts still churning over Nathaniel's death. Could he really have killed himself?

When she and Gloria had watched him from the safety of invisibility, he'd been accusing Lark of the crime. And Silas had been arrested for it already. And at the golf course, he'd practically admitted that Mr. Green's death left him in a prime position with their company. He liked the small bit of notoriety Tessa had given him.

So, why would Nathaniel admit to murdering Mr. Green when he didn't have to? He basically got off scot-free, with a lucrative company to boot.

Something didn't add up. Tessa had pretty much convinced herself that Mr. Green's son-in-law had been murdered too. But would the police think that?

She highly doubted it. The cops in Mist River seemed to like their cases straightforward, and this one was pretty much just that. If Nathaniel and Artemis had both been killed by the same person, it was going to be up to Tessa to figure out who that culprit was.

But how was she going to do that? Tessa rolled the question over and over in her mind, wondering about the best place to start with the investigation the next morning.

She tried to go back to sleep, but the thoughts were too many. Counting backward wasn't working. She was caught somewhere in the middle between dreaming and scheming her next move in tracking down this killer when several knocks rapped on her door.

Still dressed in her pajamas and struggling to figure out what time of day it was, she checked the peephole and opened the door.

"You're out of jail!"

Silas nodded. "They let me go. Someone else admitted to the crime."

"I see." Tessa knew who that someone was. She ushered Silas inside, unsure what the past few days meant for their friendship. She checked the time, and it was an unholy hour. Some people called it morning, but Tessa wasn't included with them.

Silas sat on the couch, and almost immediately, Pepper strode in, acting as if she'd had the best sleep of the century, and she leaped on the couch. She curled up next to him as he stroked her head slowly.

Tessa suddenly felt self-conscious in her pajamas. She sank into an armchair across from Silas and pulled a blanket over her. "Okay, so this is the first place you go when they release you from jail? Why? I would think you'd want to go to your *own* apartment and chill for a while. I can't imagine you got much good rest or quality food lately."

"I came here because we need to talk. While I was sitting in that cell, I had a lot of time to think about what you said—that you're the Grim Reaper—"

Tessa stiffened. "I'm not *the* Grim Reaper," she corrected. "I'm *a* grim reaper."

"Well, I believe it. I believe you. I want you to know I didn't say a word about that while I was in custody. I didn't say anything about you at all, actually, *or* the death I saw you perform."

"I didn't *perform* that death. That's not how it works. Deaths just happen the way they happen and we reapers escort the souls across the veil to the next step in their journey. We don't aid, abet, or cause deaths."

She wrinkled her nose a little as she thought about Lee Stuart. Then she shook her head to clear that particular thought. Lee hadn't killed people because he was a reaper. He'd killed people because he was a bad person.

Silas pursed his lips and seemed to mull over what she'd said in silence for a few minutes, continuing to pet Pepper, who purred softly at the attention.

Finally, he blew out a breath. "Okay, I get it. And also, that's really crazy. But I can accept it—I mean, I'm sure there are a lot of things in the world that can't be readily known or understood by the average human mind. But that's not the problem."

"No?" Tessa tried to understand where he was going with this. But her morning brain was sluggish. It would've helped if she'd had a little sleep.

"My real problem with this whole thing is that you lied to me. I knew from almost the time you took the job with Cooper's Life Insurance that something wasn't adding up. I asked you about it repeatedly. And you always lied."

Tessa winced at the pain in his voice. It was obvious she'd really hurt him.

"I can't trust you." His words were soft, but they carried a huge weight that made them sound deafening to Tessa's ears.

"Lying is not a great way to start a relationship. In fact, it's pretty much the most horrible way to start one."

He got to his feet and Tessa had to crane her neck to look up at him as he continued, "I'm not going to tell anyone your secret. But I'm also not going to get any deeper into this thing. You've made it clear you don't trust me enough to tell me the truth about things, so I'm out."

Tessa cowered into her blanket. She didn't know what to do or say. She felt like someone had hit the pause button on her.

Silas started toward the door but then stopped and turned back, pointing at Pepper. "One last thing. I'm in deep water with the owners here. I'm not sure how much longer I'll have my job. But as of now, the rules are the rules. You're not allowed to have cats in the apartment. You need to get rid of her. Today."

He covered the distance to the door in three long strides, went through, and closed it firmly behind himself while Tessa stared after him.

She groaned and rolled her head back to rest it on the back of the chair for a minute. Then she jerked it up again and looked at Pepper. "See? Even though you think you like him more than you do me, he's no friend of yours. Now you're going to have to move. And there's only one place I can take you."

Tessa threw the blanket aside and got to her feet, the fatigue of her long night setting in, draining the energy out of her body.

But she knew it was more than that. Silas' words had injured her. He was right—she *hadn't* trusted him enough to tell him the truth about her job. But somewhere deep inside, she didn't think it was fair for him to expect that of her. After all, she'd just been getting used to the fact that she was a reaper when she and Silas started flirting. How could she be expected to spill such a big thing so fast?

Still, she could understand his feelings about it too. She'd been lied to in relationships before, and it didn't feel good. In fact, it felt downright horrible. Silas was right to stop the relationship before it got any further. It wouldn't be good for either of them to stay together if he had an underlying distrust of her.

She trudged into her room, changed into jeans and a sweatshirt, and grabbed Pepper's cat carrier out of the closet.

When the cat saw the carrier, her eyes grew big, and she got to her feet, ready to leap off the couch and find a nook to hide in. But Tessa had been expecting that and grabbed Pepper before she could jump. She stuffed her, tail first, into the carrier and shut the door. Then, she peered through the grate at her angry feline friend. "Yeah, I don't blame you for not wanting to go," she said. "This is not going to be pleasant."

Chapter 14

Tessa ended up going to the coffee shop before her mother's house. While she told herself she was only doing that because her body was having a strong craving for some hot java after a basically sleepless night, the real reason was she was hoping Cheryl wouldn't be home.

She glanced at her watch. It was 7:15 AM—should be safe now. Her mother usually left the house around seven to get to the office early, while things were still quiet. She was that brand of workaholic—the kind that doesn't believe they can get real work done during work hours.

After weighing through the options, Tessa was convinced that Cheryl coming home from work and finding Pepper in her house would be better than opening the door to find her daughter standing there with a pet carrier. That thing about permission versus forgiveness.

Surely, Cheryl wouldn't scoop up the cat and throw her outside or something, once she recognized the furry girl had settled in and made herself at home.

Tessa had an idea that maybe the cat could use her old bedroom as her main place to stay. In her mind, she had it all worked out. She'd even practiced a speech to give her mother later—one in which she promised to come over daily to scoop the litter box and feed Pepper herself. "You won't have to do anything, Mom. I'll handle everything," she muttered to herself as she got out of the car and went around to the passenger side to grab the cat carrier.

Sure, it was extremely similar to something she'd said as a middle schooler when she had hoped to talk her mom into getting her a puppy. It hadn't worked then, but that didn't mean it wouldn't work now. After all, in this case she already had the cat.

And, who knew? Maybe Cheryl was lonely and would welcome the kitty in her life.

Tessa snorted out loud at that. Her mother was so prim and proper, there was almost no chance she'd be interested in having cat fur all over the place.

Tessa straightened her shoulders and headed for the house. She didn't have a choice. Silas had drawn a line in the sand when it came to Pepper, and he'd made it very clear he meant it. Tessa didn't want to antagonize him any further. Cheryl was just going to have to keep the cat, at least for a little while.

When she got to the porch, Tessa set the cat carrier on the step and slid the big orange pot full of dying petunias aside to scoop up the hidden key underneath. She unlocked the front door and left it ajar. After she returned the key and scooched the pot back into place, she grabbed Pepper again, who yowled mournfully, and stepped into the house.

"Shhh," she told the cat. "You're okay. I'll make sure you have a nice, cozy spot. You're going to love it here." She tried to keep her voice upbeat, so the cat would stay calm. But something didn't quite feel right.

Tessa realized, belatedly, the house wasn't empty. It was almost the exact opposite to how she'd felt at Nathaniel's home the previous night. Someone was walking around upstairs, and there was a light on in the kitchen.

"Mom?" Tessa called, feeling just a tiny bit uneasy about a potential intruder.

Cheryl appeared at the top of the stairs. "Tessa, what are you doing here?" She glanced at her watch. "It's pretty early for you to be awake."

No kidding.

Rolling her eyes, Tessa set the cat down a little bit behind her, sort of hoping her mother wouldn't notice. "I didn't sleep very well last night. And, um, I have a big favor to ask you."

Cheryl's forehead wrinkled.

Tessa realized she started too big. *Stall. Stall. Stall.* She pulled her hair up into a ponytail and tied it with a band she'd slipped over her wrist. "Hey, what are you still doing home, anyway? Usually, you've gone to work by this time."

Cheryl leaned to the side and returned to her previous position, now holding the handle of a suitcase. She descended the stairs with it and stopped in front of Tessa. "I'm getting ready to leave. I have . . . a business trip." Her eyes dropped to the floor and then she craned her neck to see around Tessa's shins. "What's that?" she snapped.

"It's Pepper. Silas—my landlord—says I can't keep her anymore. I don't have anywhere else to take her, so I was hoping she could stay with you."

"They let him out?"

"Yeah. It's kind of a long story." A story Tessa wasn't ready to tell.

But Cheryl had already focused her attention on the cat carrier, scowling.

Tessa held up her hands, palms out. "Just for a little while." Of course, she didn't mean that. There was nowhere else she could take Pepper, so the cat was going to have to stay with Cheryl long-term.

"I don't know. Pets aren't really my thing." Cheryl chewed her bottom lip for a second.

Tessa cocked her head, examining her mother. Cheryl had an uncharacteristic expression on her face. It was almost as though she were nervous. That was certainly not an emotion the woman exhibited very often.

Suddenly, Cheryl spun on her heel and marched to the kitchen. "Do you want some breakfast?" she called. "I'm going to scramble an egg real fast."

Tessa knelt down and peered into the cat carrier. "Stay here. I'll be back in a few minutes," she whispered.

Pepper yowled and glowered back. Tessa could almost hear her say, "Where am I supposed to go? I'm locked in."

She patted the top of the carrier as though she were patting Pepper's head, smiled, and then followed her mother into the kitchen. "Sure, I'll have an egg. Thanks."

"You don't look good, dear," Cheryl said, eyeing her daughter for a moment before heading to the refrigerator. "What happened last night?"

Tessa sank onto a bar stool and leaned on the counter. "Jake called it an emergency reap, and he explained to me a little bit, but I still don't really understand. I've never heard of such a thing."

Setting the carton of eggs on the counter, Cheryl turned to face Tessa, tipping her head. "Oh, Tessa, there's a lot to this job. Not all of it is something you can put into a manual. Things . . . change sometimes. You know, every life is different. So is every death."

Tessa felt her brow wrinkle as she tried to wrap her brain around what Cheryl had said. "Okay, but I thought all deaths were part of the universe's plan somehow. Shouldn't they be on the schedule, no matter what the cause is?"

Cheryl shook her head, pressing her lips together as she busied herself getting down a bowl and digging a whisk out of the drawer. "Not always. There are certain things—usually suicides, murders, and even some accidents—that aren't on the typical death timeline. They aren't the same as, say, a sickness that runs its course."

Cheryl paused for a moment, staring into space as though trying to figure out how to explain what she wanted to say. Then she began moving again, cracking eggs into the bowl. "It's free will, really. Humans have that, you know. Split-second decisions can be made." She grabbed the whisk and began beating the eggs, sparing a glance for her daughter.

Tessa mulled it over. "Okay," she said slowly. "So, what, some things involve free will and others don't?"

"Basically." Cheryl nodded. "Anything with less than a fifty percent chance of happening isn't reported into the reaper app. Until it becomes more than fifty percent likely. So, for example, someone with a forty-nine percent chance of committing suicide won't be reported until almost the instant it happens. The same goes for some murders."

Tessa drummed her fingers on the countertop. "But I've been involved in murder reaps before, Mom. *They* were on the app."

"Yes, because there was a greater than a fifty percent chance of them happening. Some murders are more calculated than others. Premeditation. It's really that simple. In fact, the opposite can happen too. Sometimes, we are called to a reap that doesn't end up happening. It's rare, but it does occur. It's happened to me."

Tessa didn't think it sounded simple at all, but it was at least enough of an explanation to get her started. She decided to drop the subject and bring up Pepper again, hoping to catch her mom off-guard. "You know, Pepper may not be the only one who needs somewhere to stay right now. I had a pretty major disagreement with Silas. To be honest, I'd be more comfortable not staying in my apartment right now too. Can we . . . Pepper and I . . . stay with you for a little while? We'll be quiet and neat, I promise."

Tessa crossed her fingers. If Cheryl said no, she really didn't know where else she was going to go. Maybe Gloria's house?

But Cheryl nodded. "You can stay for a little while. I'll be out of town for the rest of the week, anyway, and it will be nice to have someone housesitting." She poured the scrambled eggs into a pan she'd been warming on the stove and then turned to face Tessa while they cooked. "But you won't be able to stay for very long, I'm afraid."

I don't really want to stay that long anyway. But Tessa didn't say the thought out loud. Instead, she simply said, "Why?"

"There was something I wanted to tell you last night. But I just couldn't." Cheryl wouldn't meet her eyes. "I'm moving, and I'm selling the house. I decided to go to Chicago, so I can be closer to the main Eastern district office."

Finally, she met Tessa's eyes calmly, but Tessa could've sworn she saw a flicker of something there. What was it? If Tessa didn't know better, she would think maybe it was hope—did her mother hope Tessa would ask her not to go to Chicago?

But Tessa rejected that straight away. There was no way Cheryl would be that impractical. If she had decided that moving to Chicago was the best thing to do for her career, then she would follow that path without any concern for how Tessa may feel about it.

"That's, uh, great, Mom. I'm really proud of you for getting that promotion, and I hope you like Chicago. It will be great to come and visit you there. Maybe we can go to the museums together or something. Have some Chicago-style pizza."

Cheryl blinked a few times, and Tessa could've almost convinced herself she saw a flash of disappointment in the other woman's eyes. But she turned back toward the stove before Tessa could be sure. "Thank you, dear." She stirred the eggs and didn't say anything further.

Tessa watched her mother's back and swallowed a lump in her throat. In the space of a day, she'd lost her new boyfriend, possibly her home, and now her mother was moving away. What a rotten day. She could only hope the rest of it got better.

Chapter 15

By the time Tessa arrived at work, the sleepless night and pile-up of depressing events all weighed down on her like a physical presence. Her feet didn't seem to want to lift, and she shuffled across the asphalt and up the dilapidated sidewalk to the building.

Even the front door seemed heavy; she had to use both hands to pull it open. The effort resulted in a big yawn that forced her eyes closed and made her stumble to a stop in the lobby.

"Ooh, you look terrible. I hope it's for a fun reason." Gloria leaned on the doorjamb of her new office, appraising Tessa's condition with eyes decorated in rainbow eyeshadow. "How much did you have to drink last night?"

Tessa yawned again, not bothering to cover her mouth. "I didn't drink anything. I just didn't sleep well—or maybe not at all." She met her new boss's gaze.

A wrinkle appeared between Gloria's finely shaped eyebrows. "Wow, you really don't look good. Come on in here."

Once Tessa was inside the office with the door closed behind her, Gloria ordered, "Spill."

Tessa plummeted into a chair and then slumped down low enough that she could lean her head back on it. "Silas is free—they let him go because they had someone confess to Mr. Green's murder."

Gloria lowered herself much more gracefully into her own chair and then leaned forward. "That sounds like good news to me! Who confessed?"

"Mr. Green's son-in-law, Nathaniel. There was an emergency reap night—Jake got there before I did, but he said Nathaniel was already dead. There was a suicide note on the desk in front of him, and it said he had killed Artemis."

Gloria leaned back and slapped her thighs. "That's great! Wait, why don't you look like you think it's great news?"

"Well, for one thing, Silas is still mad at me for not telling the truth initially about being a reaper." Tessa raised her hand to keep Gloria from replying. "But mainly, the whole thing with Nathaniel and Mr. Green doesn't sit right with me."

"What do you mean? The guy killed his father-in-law, felt tremendous guilt, and committed suicide. Makes sense to me. I've seen a dozen of those true crime shows that end just like this."

"There's just something . . . I don't know. Something isn't right."

"Well, first things first—I wish you and Silas would make up already. I was hoping we could go on a double date this weekend."

Tessa shook her head. "He's super mad at me. He let me know in no uncertain terms that we're over before we really even got started. He also told me I had to get Pepper out of the apartment. So, she's at my mom's—who, by the way, is moving to Chicago. So, yeah, I don't think a double date this weekend is going to happen."

"Not with an attitude like that, it isn't." At Tessa's glare, Gloria tipped her head. ""Okay, I'm not saying all that stuff isn't a lot to deal with," Gloria admitted. "But let's start with the Silas thing. You like him, don't you?"

Tessa scrubbed a hand over her face, trying to encourage her eyes to feel more awake. "Of course I do. But the truth is that he's right. I did lie to him. He has no reason to trust me now, and I don't know how to make that up to him—how to prove that I'm not normally a liar."

"That's easy. Just have a heart-to-heart with him and explain that you didn't really want to lie to him. In fact, it was really hard for you to do it, but you thought you were supposed to. Now that you know you don't have to, everything will be A-OK."

Tessa lifted her shoulder and then let it drop back down again, which wasn't hard because she still felt the heaviness of exhaustion throughout her whole body. "Maybe. I'll think about it. But what about Mr. Green and Nathaniel?"

Gloria pulled out a handheld mirror from a desk drawer, popped it open, and started patting at her hair. "What about them? It's a police matter now. Silas has been let go, so it's really none of your concern anymore."

"Seriously? But if Nathaniel didn't kill Mr. Green—and I really don't think he did, even though I can't put my finger on why—then there's still a killer running around Mist River. Doesn't that affect us all?"

Gloria snapped the mirror shut and put it away. "We can't get involved in every suspicious thing that happens around here," she said firmly, in her newly developed boss-tone. "Our job is to escort souls across the veil, not to figure out why people died in the first place. You know our taxes pay the police force for that."

Tessa didn't answer. She just stared at her friend impassively.

Gloria blinked a few times. "I know that look. It's the same one you had in Miami. My impeccable, irrefutable logic isn't going to make a difference because you're not going to let that go, are you?"

"Probably not." Tessa's lips twitched into a smirk. "Sorry. It's my nature. I was always a curious kid."

"You're not one bit sorry. And I'm your boss now, so you should have more respect for my opinion."

Tessa put a sweet look on her face and fluttered her eyelashes. "I *do* respect you. I just don't think Mr. Green's killer should go free. Especially when it's likely that he also killed Nathaniel. Who's next?"

"You, if you aren't careful," Gloria shot back.

Tessa stared back at Gloria in silence for a moment, shocked.

Finally, her boss leaned forward and touched something sitting on her messy desk. Tessa realized it was a blank badge like the one Gloria had given her.

"I'm not giving up on this," Tessa said firmly.

"Well, if that's the case, you have everything you need to get to the bottom of it. But you're on your own. I don't want to know any more about it. Capisce?"

Tessa smiled slowly and straightened in her chair. She suddenly felt lighter than she had, the fatigue seeming to scatter to the edges of her mind. Her thoughts sharpened. "Capisce," she repeated.

Chapter 16

Tessa left Gloria's office and headed out to Linda, chewing over her next move. She knew exactly what it was—the reading of Mr. Green's will.

She'd seen the letter on Nathaniel's desk and made note of the date and time, which was in less than an hour at the Green estate. She certainly knew her way there by now. What she didn't know yet was how to get in so she could listen.

She fingered the badge, in its safe spot on the lanyard around her neck and bit her lip. She couldn't imagine the magical badge would be much help in this situation. It wasn't like she could use it to convince Mrs. Green and Hannah she belonged there.

She got in the car and sat for a moment, tapping on the steering wheel. It was too bad Corwin Blade had given her the gift of the scythe instead of invisibility. Sure, the scythe had come in handy for her once, but invisibility would be much more useful.

For a moment, she contemplated going back inside and asking Gloria to get into the reading with the invisibility magic, but she quickly decided against it. Gloria had already indicated she didn't want to have anything much to do with this investigation anymore—especially in her capacity as boss. And Tessa didn't want to test the bonds of their friendship as they were navigating this new relationship of boss and underling.

Then she remembered something. Lark's name had been on the list of beneficiaries invited to attend the reading of the will. Tessa glanced at the clock on the dashboard. She'd have to hurry, but maybe she could catch Lark before the chef went into the mansion.

As she drove across town and out toward Mr. Green's neighborhood, Tessa chuckled to herself. It was a good thing Mist River didn't have any budget issues. There were never many cops out issuing speeding tickets, and she'd been doing a lot of fast driving lately.

She was relieved when she pulled into the mouth of Mr. Green's driveway and the gate was open wide. Obviously, since they were expecting people from outside of the estate, the staff had left it unlocked.

She drove up to the house and felt even more victorious when she caught a glimpse of Lark getting out of a beat-up old Pontiac.

Tessa jumped out of Linda and hurried over to the other woman. Lark gave her a quizzical look. "Tessa. What are you doing here?"

"The lawyers at my firm believe it may be in your best interest to have representation in attendance at the reading of the will," Tessa said, doing her best to keep her tone smooth and a businesslike smile in place.

Lark scrunched her nose and then scratched it. "I don't know. Why would I need a lawyer in there now? Maybe after I know what it says."

"Oh, I'm just a paralegal. But I can sort of keep an eye on things for you, you know? If something doesn't seem like it's fair to you, I can report that right to my bosses. Then, if you need to hire them to fight anything in court for you, they'll be ready."

Tessa held her breath as Lark considered that, shifting her feet a few times and glancing toward the mansion. Her whole body stiffened. Tessa followed her gaze and caught a glimpse of Hannah standing on the porch, staring at them. But when Tessa looked at her, Hannah turned and marched into the house.

"Okay," Lark said suddenly. "Yeah, that's great. Thanks for being here."

Tessa wondered at her sudden change in attitude. Did it have something to do with Hannah? She pushed away the thought, not really caring why Lark had agreed—just glad she had.

They walked together up the stairs and through the front doorway.

Wow.

If Tessa had thought the kitchen was immaculate and grand, going through the front door was absolutely mind-blowing. She'd only ever seen such lavish decor on television. It was almost too much for her to comprehend. Elegance, fashion, and most of all, money was on full display.

Everywhere she looked, there was something that must've come from a fine Italian or French shop. Marble, glass, and brass dominated the space. At the top of an expansive, double-wide staircase with extravagantly carved railings was a gargantuan portrait of Artemis Green that looked hand-painted and must be at least six feet. He appeared serene in a forest green smoking jacket.

"This way, please." A man in a tuxedo and bowler gestured with white-gloved hands for them to head through the doorway he stood in. He was around Tessa's height but probably twenty pounds thinner, making him look almost not there. "The reading will take place in this room," he intoned, as though it were the most boring thing in the world.

Lark glanced at Tessa and then lurched forward. Tessa trailed behind, trying to see as much as she could while her eyes threatened to mutiny and squeeze shut. It was just too much extravagance to deal with at once.

When they crossed the threshold into the next room, it was only slightly less distracting. The word *sitting room* leapt to Tessa's mind as she looked around, but maybe it would've been more appropriately termed a library because book-lined shelves covered two walls. The rest of the room held several scattered seating areas, each apparently designed to provide a cozy spot to read or chat.

Tessa recognized Mrs. Green sitting in a wing-backed, burgundy chair wearing a lap blanket, her cane leaning against the square end table next to her. Hannah stood just behind her mother, resting a delicate hand on the back of the chair. Hannah's face was impassive, but Tessa caught a glimpse of red-rimmed eyes. She'd either been crying, hadn't gotten much sleep, or both.

There were a few other people in the room who Tessa didn't recognize, but by the way they were dressed and their features, she assumed they were relatives of Mr. Green—maybe nieces and nephews or, perhaps, even some of Hannah and Nathaniel's children.

Tessa followed Lark across the room, where Lark took a seat along the far wall, as though she'd chosen a spot as far away from Mrs. Green as possible. Tessa felt the elderly woman's eyes on them. When she sank onto the sofa next to Lark and looked back at Mrs. Green, she was glaring at them. But she didn't say anything, and behind her, Hannah didn't spare them a glance at all.

The tuxedoed man in the doorway bellowed once again, "This way, please." He spoke toward the front door. "The reading will take place in this room."

A moment later, a woman walked through the door. She was the no-nonsense type, wearing a navy-blue skirt suit and exactly matching pumps. Her hair was swept up into a perfect bun. She wore frameless glasses, and it was impossible to tell her age. She carried a leather suitcase, which she promptly set on an end table, opened, and withdrew papers from.

"My name is Elise Lowen, Mr. Green's estate attorney. Thank you all for coming." The crisp tone matched her businesslike demeanor and attire. "I know this is a difficult time for all of you, and I appreciate you being here for the reading of Artemis Green's will. I shall not take up much of your time."

Several of the younger crowd rushed to find seats.

Elise nodded, then glanced around the room, satisfied. "I know this is a bit unorthodox. Wills aren't usually read like this, as they are in the movies. But given the current . . . circumstances, which includes a second death in the family and the health of Mrs. Green," she inclined her head in apology to the old woman, "this is the most expedient way to proceed."

Mrs. Green waved a hand. "Yes, yes. I'm old and infirm. Everybody knows it. Have been for thirty years, at least. Get on with it, will you? I'm feeling the need to lie down soon."

Hannah patted her mother's shoulder. "It's okay, Mom. I don't think this will take too long."

Elise didn't react to Mrs. Green's rudeness. She began to read from the paper in front of her. "According to the last will and testament of Mr. Artemis Green, who was of sound mind and body when he ordered the document drawn up, his daughter Hannah is named executor of the estate."

Hannah nodded slightly, but otherwise, there was no reaction in the room. Apparently, that piece of news wasn't actually news to anyone.

The lawyer went on reading, "My wife, Mrs. Green, will maintain residence at our estate as long as she is living. She will also maintain her usual stipend from the company." Elise paused and glanced up, as though expecting questions.

Mrs. Green didn't disappoint. "What about the company?" she bellowed. "I suppose I've been named CEO?"

Elise's eyes dropped back to the paper. "Let me see. There it is. This was a more recent change. The company . . . yes, well I'd like to get back to that in a moment." She glanced back up and gave Mrs. Green a slightly reproachful look. "I'm not finished talking about the property."

Mrs. Green seemed to struggle, as though she were trying to get to her feet. She blustered and grunted for her to go on.

Hannah firmly but gently pulled her mother back into the chair and then patted her again. "It's okay, Mom. Let her read the rest. What more is there about the property?"

"Well, the deed was solely in Mr. Green's name. After Mrs. Green's death, the property is to pass to Mrs. Hannah Neilson."

Mrs. Green approved, nodding slowly. "And the company?"

Elise Lowen grimaced. There was something there she wasn't ready to read off, not even now. "Yes. The company. Here it is. The company is to pass to Ms. Lark Jordan."

Mrs. Green's mouth fell open. Around the room, murmurs went up among the various young people. It was obvious that no one had expected that.

Lark gasped and stiffened. "What?" she breathed out.

The only person besides Tessa who seemed to be taking the news calmly was Hannah. Her face was impassive, and her tone was calm when she said, "And the *other* assets? Am I to dole them out to Lark, as well?"

Elise nodded once. "Some, not all of them."

Hannah nodded and drew herself up. "Well, I hate this, but I have no choice. I must contest my father's will." She finally turned her head toward us, heat rising as splotchy red marks on her cheeks. She pointed at Lark. "Because I *know* that woman killed my husband."

Lark shot to her feet. "I did *not* kill Nathaniel or our father! I didn't even want any money *or* his company."

A rumble of footsteps in the foyer made everyone quiet down and look toward the doorway. As though on cue, several police officers entered the room.

Tessa's forehead wrinkled in confusion. It was almost as though it was staged, like they'd been waiting in the wings.

The men made a beeline for Lark.

One of the officers, a plump, red-headed man who looked no older than nineteen, squeaked, "You're under arrest for murder, ma'am. Please put your hands behind your back and turn around slowly."

"What? No! I didn't kill anyone. I couldn't!" Tears streamed down Lark's face. Then her expression hardened, and she scowled at Hannah. "I wouldn't be surprised if you did it. You always did want to keep everything to yourself."

Hannah marched over and stood a few feet away from Lark. "You should have left this family alone while you had the chance. But no. You had to stick your nose in where you weren't wanted. There was no way you could ever have what we have unless you killed to get it."

"You know that's not true!"

"Now you're going to have nothing—less than nothing—just like you deserve." Hannah looked at the officer, who had finished handcuffing Lark. "Take her out of *my* home," she spat before whirling around and stomping back to her mother.

As they began to pull her from the room, Lark cast a panicked glance over her shoulder at Tessa. "I'm going to need the help from your law firm that you promised me before," she called before disappearing through the doorway.

Tessa winced. *Right. The law firm. The very fake law firm.*

Chapter 17

Tessa jabbed at the screen of her cell phone, sending off a quick SOS text to Gloria that explained what happened at the reading as a vision of Lark's panicked face floated in her mind. Then, she leaned against Linda's driver-side door.

So much for keeping Gloria out of it. She'd messed up. Badly. First, she'd managed to get Silas into big trouble, and now Lark had been hauled away to jail. Not only that, but Lark also thought she had a connection with real lawyers, and she didn't because Tessa had lied.

What was she thinking? She shouldn't have used that ruse to get into Lark's home to talk to her or to get into the reading of the will.

Tessa had always thought she was a good person. One who told the truth. Before she became a grim reaper, she'd done nothing more than the occasional little white lie here and there. Sometimes, she would tell elderly ladies like Mrs. Cross she liked their hair instead of telling them the style came and went in the Eighties. Tessa considered herself ethical, moral, and decent. But lately, the lies were piling up, and people were getting hurt because of them.

She should have let this whole thing go, just like Gloria said. After Silas was cleared of Mr. Green's murder, she should've let the whole matter go. There was no way she could solve this case. She didn't even have a right to try.

Misery seemed to soak into every cell in her body. Remorse and guilt warred with embarrassment in her thoughts.

She checked her phone screen, but Gloria hadn't answered yet. What was she going to be able to do about it anyway? Tessa had gotten herself and others into this mess—why should her friend need to get involved, wade into the lies and mistakes, and bail her out?

But she had no idea what to do next—or how to fix this.

She heard the mansion's front door start to open and, on a whim, dashed around the back of Linda, crouching low in the bushes. There were still a few stray cars in the driveway from the reading, so Tessa hoped whoever was coming out wouldn't recognize her old Buick.

She peered around the car's back fender and saw Hannah coming outside with an officer. They were chatting in low tones, but Tessa couldn't hear what they were saying. She wanted to get closer.

The pair descended the porch steps and then headed around the house, and Tessa scurried forward, mindful of the cameras on the corners of the house. She may not be good at keeping her friends out of trouble, but Tessa had proven to be fairly talented at staying in the shadows. She really wanted to know what Hannah and the detective were talking about.

As they approached the back end of the house, Hannah and the officer continued toward the horse paddock. Tessa put on a burst of speed to get closer, and she could finally hear them.

"That's a big favor I just did for you," the detective said. "We don't really have much evidence against Lark."

Hannah leveled a cool look at her companion. "Well, this gives you time to find it. I told you, and your handwriting expert will verify it, that the note Nathaniel left wasn't written in his handwriting. That signature looked like his but not the rest."

The detective kicked at a stone in his path, and it tumbled up the gravel lane ahead of them. "Assuming you're right, that doesn't mean it was Lark's handwriting."

Hannah crossed her arms over her chest, as though her sleeves weren't thick enough to keep out the autumn chill. "That's true. But just think about it for a minute. Who else had a motive to murder my father?"

The detective stopped in his tracks and barked out a laugh. "Well, I can think of a few people." His tone was sarcastic as he inclined his head toward Hannah and gave her a pointed look.

"You've got to be kidding me!" She kept walking, and the officer lengthened his strides to catch back up with her. "When my father died, I was with my husband, and when Nathaniel died, I was here with my mother. She often needs help during the night, and I don't trust the staff enough to leave her alone with them."

"Did she need you last night?"

"No. Mom took a sleeping pill and slept through the night. She even slept in a little, which isn't like her. This whole affair is weighing heavily on her."

They walked in silence for a while until they arrived at the fence line. Hannah put her hands on top and stared out into the paddock. Then she made a kissing noise with her mouth, and several horses looked up from where they had been munching. Slowly, they began to make their way over to her.

The officer didn't touch the fence, and he didn't look at the horses. His attention was on Hannah. "What about this Silas

St. Onge guy? The one we originally arrested. Where does he come in?"

She shrugged and held out her hand for the first horse who arrived, a chestnut gelding. He whinnied a greeting and then grabbed the carrot out of her hand. "I don't know Silas. Why?"

The officer took half a step away from the fence, as though he were slightly afraid of the horse. He kept an eye on the creature as he spoke. "We believe he may have been planted by someone. You know, to take the fall. He wouldn't say why he was here that morning, only that he was a fan of Mr. Green and trying to catch a glimpse."

Hannah's head whipped around, and she pinned the officer with a hard look. "You know we've had folks like that before."

"Yeah, well, we've got him under surveillance now. Is that thing dangerous?" He gestured toward the horse.

Hannah laughed. "Of course not. He's as gentle as they come. Would you like to take a ride?"

Tessa crept away, guilt an even more crushing presence than it had been a moment before.

Silas was under surveillance? This was all her fault.

Well, there was one silver lining in what she'd managed to find out. The police knew Nathaniel hadn't committed suicide.

As she arrived back in the driveway, Tessa's phone buzzed, and she pulled it out to see the text from Gloria: *Meet me at the police station. I have a plan.*

Chapter 18

When Tessa pulled up outside the police station, she thought for a moment that her mom was waiting in front of the building for her. After a second, she realized it was Gloria, dressed in a pantsuit.

Tessa jumped out of Linda and hurried over to Gloria. She gestured toward the outfit. "Not really your style, is it?"

"I borrowed it from Ella. She works for a CPA. Just trust me, all right, and trust our badges to get us through." She headed toward the door, and Tessa followed along, clutching the badge on her lanyard.

They approached the front desk inside the police station, which was behind a layer of bulletproof glass. Gloria rapped on it to get the attention of the desk sergeant, whose back was turned as he stood waiting for a Keurig to finish dripping coffee into a black mug with a Star Trek logo. He glanced over his shoulder but didn't come toward them until the cup was full. Then he carried it over and slid open a circular piece of glass to talk through. "How can I help you ladies this morning?"

"We represent Lark Jordan, and we'd like to speak with our client alone. Right now. You've kept her here long enough without representation." Gloria's tone was firm.

The officer looked nonplussed. "She had her phone call," he said. "Used it to call her mom. She did say her lawyers should be showing up, though. Hang on, I'll come around." He snapped the hole shut, grabbed his coffee mug, and disappeared out the back of the office. Moments later, he reappeared in the lobby and gestured for them to follow him through the open door.

Gloria and Tessa glanced at each other as they followed the man down a short hallway. Gloria gave Tessa a thumbs-up, and she returned it halfheartedly, wondering how much time one could get in jail for impersonating a lawyer. Probably a lot.

The officer left them in a tiny room that was barely big enough to hold its rectangular table and four rickety wooden chairs. After a few moments, he dumped Lark into the room as well. Gesturing toward a panel on the wall, he said, "I'm going to lock the door. When you're done, use the intercom to call, and I'll be here to let you out."

After he was gone, Gloria stuck out her hand to Lark. "I'm Blanche Stewart. We need to have a little talk and get some facts straight about your case."

Lark's eyes flitted over to Tessa, and she wrung her hands. "Okay," she said in a small voice.

Tessa noticed Gloria didn't specifically tell Lark she was a lawyer, and she hadn't used the word with the desk sergeant either.

Lark sat down across from the two non-lawyers. Gloria leaned back in her chair. "I assume you're going to tell me you didn't kill Artemis Green or Nathaniel Neilson," she said.

"That's exactly what I'm going to tell you because it's true. There's no way I would've killed my dad. He and I had a great relationship."

"Okay, Tessa tells me that you worked for Mr. Green and that he knew you were his daughter. Have we got it right so far?"

Lark nodded. "My mom worked for the Greens first, for many years. She'd take me to work with her, so I could see my dad. I also played with my half-sister, Hannah, all the time. It was really neat—I sort of got to grow up with her, even though she didn't know we were truly sisters." A troubled look flitted over her eyes.

Gloria leaned in closer. "I feel like you're holding something back."

Lark winced. "I did try to tell her one time—"

"Really? How did that go?" Gloria shifted in her chair, clearly interested in this answer.

"She was angry. Called me a liar. From that moment on, she hated me. I completely ruined our relationship when I tried to tell her the truth." Lark sniffed as though trying to hold back tears. "I guess it must've come as a big shock to her after Dad died, to find out I was really telling the truth."

Tessa's mind raced at this new information. Hannah hated Lark, but she'd known the closely guarded secret. The puzzle pieces fell together. Hannah must've found out that Artemis had changed his will and knew the only way to keep her full inheritance was to frame Lark for the murder, so she would be disallowed from receiving the business. But Silas being there and getting arrested had put a wrench into her plans.

It all made sense except for one thing—would she really have killed Nathaniel too? Why would she have done that?

Gloria and Lark were still talking, but Tessa wasn't listening anymore. She chewed over the problem in her mind. Had Nathaniel actually killed Mr. Green and then Hannah killed him to keep the secret? She supposed that made sense. Hannah was his wife, so she would've had the best access to him that night, plus it would be easy for her to say that the handwriting on the suicide note wasn't his.

It was hard for her to believe someone would kill their own father and husband, but she remembered Hannah's impassive, non-emotional face at the reading of the will, and a chill went up her spine.

"I guess I'm going to miss my dad's funeral this afternoon," Lark lamented, and Tessa's attention snapped back to her.

"Where is it?"

Lark shrugged. "Where else? At the estate. Mrs. Green doesn't go out—hasn't for a long time. He's being buried in the private cemetery on the grounds."

"What time is the funeral?"

"Two," Lark answered.

Tessa checked her watch—it was 12:30. She'd have to hurry.

She cut her eyes to Gloria, and her friend nodded. "You go. I'll handle things here."

Tessa jumped to her feet and crossed the room to hit the intercom button as Gloria and Lark continued to speak softly. She waited impatiently for the officer to come let her out. It seemed like forever. She bounced impatiently on the balls of her feet and checked her watch every ten seconds. Finally, he appeared.

It took her a moment to explain to him that Gloria was staying but that she was ready to go. He finally let her out into the hallway and then relocked the door.

Tessa followed him back out to the lobby, but as he was opening the door, the handle flew out of his hand. A man on the other side had opened it at the same time. Tessa recognized him as the detective who had been afraid of the horses at the Green estate.

Recognition lit up his face as well. "You were at the will reading with Lark Jordan. Oh, you must be her representation."

At least the guy was observant, like a detective should be.

"My firm is," she corrected. "I'm just a paralegal."

He nodded and looked strangely pleased to find out she wasn't a lawyer. "I'm still working on that investigation," he said. "Just trying to figure out the truth here."

"Good," Tessa said. "I'd hate to think the detectives on the case were just taking everything at face value."

"You got something to tell me?" he asked, studying her closely.

She shook her head. "Not yet, anyway."

He pulled out a billfold from his back pocket and scrounged around in it for a minute before producing a business card, which he handed to her. "Well, if that changes, give me a call right away." He shook his head and looked thoughtful. "Nathaniel Neilson had a strange cocktail of drugs in his system," he said.

Tessa tipped her head. "Really? Like what?"

He shrugged. "Sleeping pills, for sure. There was some other stuff there too—not the common stuff like street drugs or Tylenol or something. The crime lab had to send a blood sample to a private lab with the capability of doing more detailed testing. We're still waiting on the report to find out exactly what the other substances were."

Now *that* was interesting. Tessa zoned out for a minute, trying to figure out what that meant.

Then she checked her watch again. "Oops. Gotta go." She held up the business card. "Thanks for this." Halfway across the lobby, she turned to find him still standing there, watching her. "Keep your phone close this afternoon, okay?

Chapter 19

Tessa jogged across the parking lot of Mist River Manor. Another glance at her watch told her she only had about forty-five minutes to get to the funeral in time, and she needed to change clothes. When the building's front door opened, she had a premonition of who would be coming through it, but she hoped to be wrong. She didn't have the time or inclination to deal with him at that moment.

But she was going to have to. It was Silas.

She'd always heard of people having long faces when they were sad or upset about something, but she never actually fully understood what it meant until seeing Silas in that moment. It was as though gravity was pulling on his facial features harder than it normally did. Like he was in a bubble that applied two G's instead of the regular one.

Tessa came to a stop. There was no way she could get past him and into the apartment building without acknowledging his existence because he was staring right at her. "Hi," she said. "Is everything okay?"

She knew it wasn't. And she knew without a shadow of a doubt that she'd played some hand in it. She was a one-woman wrecking ball.

Silas shook his head and stuffed his hands into his jean pockets. "Nope. I got booted out of my job today." He shook his head and looked at the ground. "I've worked hard here for years. One mistake and I get let go. I still can't believe it."

Tessa drew herself up, feeling shocked and scandalized on his behalf. "That's not fair!"

He shrugged, and at the end of it, his shoulders slumped even lower than they did before. "Yeah, well, life's not fair, is it?"

Tessa winced. "Silas, I'm so sorry. About everything. You were totally right—I should've trusted you with my secret. Then you wouldn't have needed to follow me to Artemis Green's house. This is all on me."

His eyes bounced up, and his gaze met hers. His features softened. "No, I get it now. It's a *big* secret, and I came on too strong. I never should've expected you to reveal something like that to me when we were just getting to know each other. I should've focused on the romance."

She smiled. "I wish you would've."

He pulled one hand out of its pocket and pushed a flop of hair out of his eyes. "I don't know what gets into me sometimes. I can just be so—" He paused, as though trying to figure out the right word, and then unexpectedly burst into laughter. "Well, my mom would've said bull-headed. I guess that's pretty close to right. I am a Taurus, after all."

Tessa was relieved to see him smiling. Her eyes moved toward the door behind Silas.

His gaze followed. "Where are you off to? Pepper need some food?"

She raised her eyebrows.

He shrugged. "I don't have to worry about you having a cat anymore. Get a whole litter for all I care. In fact, you should. Give the owner's new landlord hire a run for their money."

Tessa shook her head. "No. I took Pepper to my mom's house. But I do have to get going. I'm in a rush right now." Another glance at her watch made her suck in a breath and take a step around Silas.

"Oh. I see. Something for . . . you know what?" He leaned closer and whispered, "The reaper stuff?"

"Sorta."

He held up a hand. "Fair enough. I'm not going to be sticking my nose in where it's not wanted in that area ever again." He reached over and brushed a piece of hair off her cheek.

The touch sent a jolt through her, and Tessa's heartrate picked up.

Silas stuffed the hand back into his pocket, as though trying to keep it from doing something he didn't want it to. "Romance," he said. "I'm sticking with romance. Would you be interested in going out to dinner with me again? Clean slate. No reaper talk."

"Seriously?"

A line appeared between his brows. "I understand if you don't want to. I was an idiot, and it would serve me right if you told me to get lost and stop bothering you. If you do, I'll disappear, and you won't have to worry about me again."

She couldn't stop a huge smile from spreading across her face.

But Silas didn't see it because he was staring at the ground again. "Actually, never mind. Forget I asked. You don't need to answer . . ."

Tessa put a hand on his arm and squeezed. "Silas!"

He raised his eyes to meet hers. "Yeah?"

"I'd love to."

"Really?"

"Absolutely. Text me later, and we'll figure out a time. I have to get going right now."

Tessa's mind had already jumped ahead to her apartment, thinking about the black dress in the back of the closet that she'd change into. Not only was it funeral-appropriate, but it was also good for keeping to the shadows.

"Great. I'll do that," Silas said as she gave him one last wave on the way into the building.

Tessa dug through her purse for the apartment keys as she hurried across the lobby, trying to figure out which shoes to wear with the dress.

When she got to the door, there was a Post-It note stuck over the peep hole.

Weird.

She yanked it down, barely registering the words that told her a package too big for her mailbox was being held at the front desk. The handwriting wasn't Silas's, like it normally would be. It was a different person's scrawl, and something about it jolted a thought loose in her brain.

She paused with the key in the door, staring at the Post-It.

"Well, I'll be . . ." she whispered.

She stuffed the Post-It into her purse and then made sure Detective Taggert's card was safe and in an accessible spot. If her new thought panned out, she'd be needing to use his number soon.

Then, she exploded into her apartment, even more eager than before to change and get to Artemis Green's funeral.

Chapter 20

There were a lot of people at the funeral. Like, a lot. Tessa had barely made it in time, as the tuxedoed, bowler-hatted butler let her know in no uncertain terms as he led her to a large room on the second floor of the mansion and dropped her off with a final judgmental sniff.

Regardless of the attitude the butler had thrown her, there was still a crowd of people filtering slowly through the door, so she wasn't unforgivably late. Still, her mother wouldn't have approved.

Tessa got on her tiptoes to peek into the room. The funeral was being held in a ballroom with burgundy and silver carpet, high ceilings, and an elaborate chandelier that definitely looked like it had come from Europe and probably was centuries old. Tessa had to drag her attention away from the surroundings to focus on the people around her. They all spoke in the hushed tones that befit such an event, but she caught snippets of conversation that made it clear Mr. Green had been very well-liked in the community.

Tessa hadn't moved very far in line when louder voices erupted ahead. She rose on her toes again and caught a glimpse of Hannah in the doorway, arms crossed, barring Sky from entering. "You aren't welcome here." Her voice sounded like stones hitting each other. "Please leave."

She couldn't hear Sky's answer, but Tessa decided it was the perfect opportunity. She scooched around people, threading her way through the crowd and through the doorway while everyone else's attention was on the argument.

Tessa found a chair near the back of the room, hoping she could just blend in with the crowd. She scanned the pamphlet the butler had reluctantly handed her and made a note that the plan was for everyone to accompany the casket to the gravesite after a short service and before returning to the mansion for a catered luncheon. Tessa knew that would be her chance to enact the crazy plan she'd drummed up.

The room quieted as Hannah helped her mother to the front row. Sky had disappeared.

A minister began to speak into a microphone, talking about Mr. Green's childhood. Tessa caught sight of Mrs. Cross in the second row, just behind Hannah and Mrs. Green. She kept blowing her nose into a bright yellow handkerchief.

Tessa didn't have a great view of Mrs. Green or her daughter, but when Hannah cast a glare back at Mrs. Cross, it was evident that her eyes were red-rimmed.

Even though she tried to keep her attention on the service, Tessa didn't hear much of it. Her thoughts kept swirling back to cover bits of information related to the deaths of Artemis and Nathaniel, now that she had a new lens through which to examine them.

Once the service was over and people began to file out of the room, Tessa inserted herself into the center of the crowd and left with them. But when everyone else headed downstairs, she darted upstairs as fast as possible and slipped into the first small, empty room she came across.

It was a small bedroom, but it didn't take long for Tessa to determine it was just for guests. She stuck her head into the hallway, didn't see anyone, and sprinted to the next room. After checking out six or seven rooms that way, Tessa finally arrived at a set of heavy oak double doors carved with birds, flowers, and butterflies, at the end of a hallway.

This has got to be it!

She cracked the door open.

The room was huge, with a four-poster bed covered in elegant fabrics the various colors of a summer sunset. Tessa entered the room and closed the door behind her. She crossed the floor quickly, passing a hand-carved wooden structure that held five or six different canes. That let her know she was in the right place—Mrs. Green's private quarters.

Tessa made a beeline for the huge, delicately carved walnut desk facing a huge window that overlooked the horse pasture. She moved papers around, looking at each one of them carefully but swiftly. But there was nothing there.

She turned in a slow circle, examining the room closely but not sure what she was looking for. Her fingers tapped a beat on the desk as she bit her lip.

Her fingers hit something that felt different from the rest of the desk, and Tessa glanced down, expecting to see a mouse pad or blotter. She frowned. It was a slight divot in the surface of the wood. She probed at it and squeaked when a tiny panel moved under her fingers.

A noise across the room made Tessa spin around. She caught the last bit of movement as a narrow floor-to-ceiling armoire slid aside to reveal an equally narrow doorway.

She glanced back at the panel on the desk. "Cool," she breathed before hurrying over to the door. Her fingers trembled just a touch as she twisted the knob and prayed it wouldn't be locked. It gave under her hand. "Yes!"

Tessa cracked open the door and peeked in.

It was a stairwell.

She left the door open because light from the big window splashed in enough that she could see a little. She crept forward, but before she got to the stairs, which led downward, something caught her eye. She pulled out her phone and swiped up, then tapped the flashlight icon. When it came on, she pointed it at the pile of jugs at the top of the stairs.

Bingo.

Tessa snapped several pictures and then pulled out Detective Taggert's business card. She texted him the pictures and then hurried back through the secret doorway.

For a second, it was too bright in the room, and she stumbled to a halt and blinked several times, trying to adjust.

When her vision cleared, she started, took two steps, and then jerked to a stop again. She sucked in a breath and held up her hands. "Don't shoot," she said.

Chapter 21

Mrs. Green stood in the doorway, straight, without a cane. She looked at least ten or fifteen years younger than she had downstairs during the funeral. She held the gun pointed at Tessa, with no hint of trembling in her arm. A sneer twisted her face. "I saw you that morning, you know," she said. "You were with that boy—that fan of Artemis's who was arrested and then released."

Tessa felt her eyebrows twitch upward and struggled to keep her expression impassive while her mind swirled around, frantically trying to figure out how to get out of this one. The only thing she could think of at the moment was to draw out the conversation. "You saw me?"

Mrs. Green barked out a short laugh. "Oh, there isn't much the security cameras around this house don't pick up if you know which ones to check, like I do. I used them to keep tabs on my daughter and that Lark when they were younger and, later, my daughter and her good-for-nothing boyfriend, Nathaniel. Oh, yes, I recognized you at the reading of the will, and I knew there was something strange going on. I knew you were after something."

"I'm after the truth," Tessa said flatly.

"I'll tell you the truth," she snapped. "But it isn't pretty. A young lady like you will surely think I'm the monster of the story."

Tessa didn't answer. Even though she didn't want to show weakness, she also knew it was a bad idea to antagonize the woman with the gun.

There was one other way she could end the conversation. She could call on the power of the scythe. But here and now, it didn't feel right. She wasn't judge, jury, or executioner—no matter what Silas thought of her career. There had to be some other way of talking sense into Mrs. Green.

The old lady twisted her hips to sidestep the door as she swung it shut behind her. She laughed at Tessa's widened eyes, misinterpreting the reaction. "I see you're surprised at how well I can get around. The truth is, my condition has improved over the years. I'm feeling much better. Much, much better. My husband spent millions on my rehabilitation, and it did the trick. He just never knew it."

"Why hide it?" Tessa demanded.

"Ha! Because I wanted my husband to think I was infirm. I needed him to continue to provide for me. If he'd known I wasn't sick, he would have divorced me. Left me with a measly stipend and a regular house in the suburbs."

Tessa shook her head. "Why would he do that?"

"Because, over the years, we drifted apart—oh, I knew he had an affair with Sky Jordan. Of course, I knew. Just like I knew the brat of a child she brought around here was his daughter. I saw how he played with her and smiled at her when he didn't think I was watching. The look in his eyes, why, it was the exact same one he gave our own daughter.

"Over the years, I watched that man dangle his mistress and her daughter right in front of my face and Hannah's too. As though he thought I was stupid. Just a stupid, old, crippled wife that he felt good about taking pity on and keeping around." She sneered again, and it twisted her features into something much darker.

Tessa realized the woman had marinaded in her own spite and anger for decades. *How sad.* "Do you really think your husband felt that way about you?"

"What would you know about it? You're still young, with your looks about you. You have no idea what it's like to be married for so many years and then get sick—to be unable to go on trips with your husband or host the parties he wants you to." The corners of her lips plunged downward. "To watch your husband get bored and go elsewhere."

For a second, Tessa felt sorry for her, but somehow, she knew the old woman wouldn't appreciate sympathy. She pressed her lips together.

Mrs. Green went on, a faraway look in her eyes, as though she'd forgotten Tessa was there. "Oh, he didn't say he was bored. He said he was *lonely*. Whined that I shut him out when I got sick—that I treated him like a stranger. What a load of ridiculousness. He was just making excuses for his transgressions. But I knew—oh, I knew what they were. I never let on to him that I knew, but I did. And I also knew that he would give some of his fortune to that illegitimate daughter when he died. Some of the wealth that was rightfully *my* daughter's."

"So, you killed him because of the changes to his will?"

"I *wanted* to kill him before he made the changes," she said gruffly. "But the opportunity never presented. When I found out he'd already been to his lawyer, I had to change my plan. Make it look like Lark had done the deed, so she wouldn't be able to receive the inheritance. I used my hidden stairwell." She waved a hand toward the doorway where I'd found the jugs of cleaner already. "Way back in the day, before

Artemis had this place basically rebuilt from the ground up, that was a servant's stairway. It was a way for the kitchen staff to bring food and drink directly to the master room—quicker than going through the rest of the house, so they could attend to the needs of their employers efficiently. Over the years, everyone forgot it was there except for me. But then you and that fan boy had to go and screw everything up. It delayed Lark's arrest."

Tessa gave her that. Silas's bout of espionage had put a wrench in a lot of things. But it didn't explain everything. She squinted at Mrs. Green. "Why did you kill Nathaniel, then?"

"Well, once I had my way, Hannah was to inherit everything. But she would have let that worthless son-in-law of mine take control of things. She was never a leader. Not like I was in my youth. That was before my ailment.

"No. Hannah always preferred to defer to her husband. And he would've driven our business and her fortune into the ground. I never did like him, and neither did Artemis. It was one of the few things we agreed on during the last twenty years of our marriage. Is that enough truth for you, girl?" Mrs. Green took several steps forward, re-aiming the gun to make sure it was centered on Tessa's chest. The floor squeaked under her feet.

Desperately, Tessa tried to figure out how to keep the woman talking. "You don't really want to do this." She put a note of pleading into her tone that she hoped would draw Mrs. Green's attention.

In her purse, though she had turned the phone down as low as it would go, she recognized the annoying buzz of the emergency reap alert. Her heart rate skyrocketed. Was the emergency reap for her? Which one of the agency's reapers would come to help her cross the veil?

Mrs. Green put a sweet smile on her face. "Oh, you're trespassing. I'm well within my rights to shoot you. I'll simply tell them you were up here trying to steal jewelry, and when I walked in on you, you attacked me."

The floor squeaked again.

But Mrs. Green hadn't moved. Confusion crossed her face, and she turned to look over her shoulder.

Tessa surged forward, crouching low in case Mrs. Green pulled the trigger. She crashed into the old woman's knees, and they both went down. The gun flew out of Mrs. Green's hand. Her knee came up, nailing Tessa in the solar plexus. She wasn't kidding about her rehabilitation.

Tessa gasped for air, folding into a fetal position. Mrs. Green inched across the floor toward the gun.

Fighting through the pain and lack of oxygen, Tessa wrenched herself around. She had to get to the gun before Mrs. Green if she wanted to live.

But as they both reached for the weapon, Tessa knew she was too late. Mrs. Green was an inch closer.

Just before the elderly woman's wrinkled hand could close on the pistol's handle, the gun moved on its own, away from her grasp.

Tessa craned her neck to watch the gun float from the floor up into the air. Mrs. Green gaped like a fish trying to get oxygen out of the air on a boat deck. "What? Who? What?" she sputtered.

But Tessa knew exactly who was in that invisible space. Gloria didn't address Mrs. Green. Instead, her words were meant for Tessa. "I guess I was the closest reaper around when the emergency reap alert went off. I was meant to take you across the veil. But that would have been a lot of paperwork, and I'm just getting started in management, so I thought I'd buy you some time until the cavalry arrives instead."

As though on cue, the soft sound of sirens floated through the air. Gloria helped Tessa to her feet. The invisible reaper and the gun headed down the hidden stairwell.

Mrs. Green pushed herself to a sitting position. She was back to looking old and frail, her expensive clothes rumpled and her hair wisping loose from its braid. "I hope you don't think you're done with me," she hissed at Tessa.

"Oh, I don't," Tessa answered. "Somehow, I'm positive you and I will be crossing paths again soon. Very soon. But I'll probably be working in my official capacity when that happens."

Chapter 22

Silas helped Tessa out of his pick-up truck with a strong, warm hand, and they crossed the parking lot together. "I've been wanting to try this place," he said. "Good call on the restaurant choice."

Tessa could almost taste the pad thai already. "I hope they have good spring rolls. That's how I judge Thai restaurants."

Gloria waited by the place's front door, arm-in-arm with another woman. Gloria wore spiked heels that sent her soaring over everyone but Silas, and that was close.

Tessa admired Gloria's miniskirt and embroidered pink shirt. "Much better than the pant suit." She grinned.

Gloria rolled her eyes. "I'll take that as a thank you for being the best boss ever and saving your behind more than once." She winked. "This is Ella."

Tessa beamed at the blonde, who wore her hair in two braids and sported huge round glasses. They shook hands, and Tessa could already feel a kinship. She threw an arm around Ella and headed into the restaurant. "So, tell me. What's it like to date Gloria? She's super bossy, right?"

Unfortunately, Ella wouldn't give Tessa any good dirt. She merely smiled and kept repeating that Gloria was lovely and had no bad habits.

Once they had their drinks and had ordered food, Gloria regarded Tessa. "I heard the cops found footage of Mrs. Green leaving the house the night Nathaniel died."

Tessa took a sip of ice water and nodded. "I had to give Detective Taggert a nudge on that one, but they found it eventually. She took the golf cart Mr. Green had used to get around the property, heading in the direction of Hannah and Nathaniel's house. Between that and the cleaner in her secret passageway, there's enough to charge her."

"Great instincts, finding that hidden stairwell and that stuff," Gloria said. "How'd you know to look for it?"

Heat burned Tessa's cheeks. "I didn't. I was actually looking for some evidence that Mrs. Green had practiced Nathaniel's handwriting. When I saw a Post-It note on my apartment door, written by someone other than Silas, who usually writes them, I remembered Hannah saying the suicide note wasn't in her husband's handwriting. Then, I remembered something Mrs. Cross told me about Mrs. Green—that after she got sick, she spent a lot of time inside practicing calligraphy. That's when I realized she must have killed Nathaniel."

Gloria held up her glass for Tessa to clink. "Well, cheers. Glad that's over. As your new boss, I'd like to request that you stay out of any future murder investigations, okay?"

"Okay." Mentally, Tessa was crossing her fingers behind her back. Physically, her fingers were laced with Silas's.

"I really do want to avoid extra paperwork." Gloria pursed her lips. "Besides, I'm going to have to focus on finding and training a new reaper to take my place. That should be fun."

"How does one find a new reaper?" Tessa wondered aloud. She made a mental note that Ella knew their real job. She wasn't surprised, after the way Gloria had encouraged her to be truthful with Silas about it. "I think my mom chose me just because I was desperate for a job and she didn't want me to move in with her."

Everyone laughed. The smile stayed on Gloria's lips as she answered. "Well, there are a lot of ways to go about it. But, generally, if there is someone around who already knows about reapers and has proven themselves to have good values and a stellar work ethic, that's where we start." Her gaze slid over to land on Silas.

Shock coursed through Tessa, making her feel weak for a second. She set the water glass down.

But Silas didn't look surprised. He just gazed back at Tessa, calm as could be.

"Wait, you already offered him the job?" Tessa asked.

"Yep."

Tessa's head whipped around to Silas. "And you said yes?"

He held out his hands. "I'm kind of in a tight spot," he said. "I've already been looking for maintenance jobs, but the pickings are pretty slim." He shrugged. "If you don't want me to accept, I understand."

Tessa drew in a breath and thought about it for a minute. Was it a good idea to mix romance and work?

Probably not.

But Silas's expression, even though it was obvious he was trying to keep it blank, held a hint of pleading. He really wanted to do it. Who was she to block him from being a reaper?

"Congratulations!" She squeezed his hand. "You'll be an awesome reaper."

Relief skipped over his features. "I hope so."

"Aw! How sweet," Ella sighed and leaned into her girlfriend.

"Yeah. Lovebirds who get to be co-workers too." She put on a fake stern expression and pointed at Tessa and Silas. "I expect you to be professional and get along. Souls come first," she chided.

Tessa nodded along with Silas. Yeah. They could make it work. It was going to be fine. Maybe even fun.

She pushed away thoughts of working with Frank and how *not* well that had gone. Silas wasn't Frank. He was everything Frank wasn't. Someone she wanted to take home.

Everything would be okay.

***

The next Monday, Tessa made it a point to get to work early. It was Silas's first day on the job, and she wanted to be there before him.

She was surprised to see her mother in the lobby when she walked in. "Oh. Hi. What are you doing here?"

Cheryl gestured to a cardboard box on the floor next to her. "Just grabbing the last of my things." She glanced at her watch. "You're here early."

"I'm turning over a new leaf," Tessa said. "I'm nose-to-the-grindstone girl now."

Cheryl smirked. "Big plans. Good luck with that." She tapped perfect red nails on the reception desk. "You're doing a good job, you know," she said finally. "I'm proud of you."

Woah. "Thanks, Mom." There was more she wanted to say, but the words didn't want to come. There hadn't been many times in Tessa's life when Cheryl had verbalized her feelings so clearly. It felt . . . good.

But the moment was over quickly. Cheryl turned away, flipping through some papers on the desk. "I did do a little something for you. Consider it a gift before I go."

"Really? What'd you do?"

Cheryl glanced at Tessa and then away again. "I used the reaper secret Mr. Blade gave me years ago to smooth things over for you and Silas."

Excitement spiked in Tessa's chest. Cheryl had alluded to the fact that she'd been given a gift from the Grim Reaper but refused to say what it was. "What does that mean?"

"I cleared your and Silas's involvement in the murder case from the minds of the officers and those involved."

Tessa's jaw dropped. "Wait. You can wipe people's memories?"

Cheryl grinned. "Yes."

"Wow. That's so cool." Tessa mulled it over for a minute, considering how that gift could really come in handy for a reaper agency. Then a thought occurred to her, and her eyes widened. "Wait, did you ever use that on me?"

Cheryl's eyebrows twitched upward a fraction, but she didn't answer. Instead, she said, "I considered letting Mrs. Green remember what she heard and saw but that would likely have landed her in a psych ward. I'd rather see her in jail for murdering two people, so I wiped her memory too."

"Mom . . ." Tessa's tone was suspicious.

"What?" Cheryl wore an innocent look. "Wouldn't you like to thank me? I couldn't have our new reaper starting out in hot water with the local police department."

Tessa heard a car door close. A glance outside revealed that Silas was on his way inside.

Cheryl finally pushed away the papers and faced her daughter. "And the only hot water you're in now, Theresa, is with me."

"What? Why am I in trouble with you?" Tessa wondered if Pepper had done something destructive in the house. Of course, she was going to have to find somewhere else to live soon because it was already up for sale, and Tessa couldn't have Pepper at the apartment anymore. Silas was looking for a new place too.

"Because you haven't bothered to introduce me to your new boyfriend," Cheryl said with a smile.

Tessa barked out a laugh as Silas came through the door. He looked handsome and ready to tackle his new life. "Well, let's fix that, shall we?"

Also By Christine Zane Thomas

Witching Hour starring 40 year old witch Constance Campbell

Book 1: Midlife Curses[1]

Book 2: Never Been Hexed[2]

Book 3: Must Love Charms[3]

Book 4: You've Got Spells[4]

Tessa Randolph Cozy Mysteries written with Paula Lester

Grim and Bear It[5]

The Scythe's Secrets[6]

Reap What She Sows[7]

Foodie File Mysteries starring Allie Treadwell

The Salty Taste of Murder[8]

A Choice Cocktail of Death[9]

A Juicy Morsel of Jealousy[10]

The Bitter Bite of Betrayal[11]

---

1. https://alsoby.me/r/amazon/B085GJLYCF?fc=us&ds=1

2. https://alsoby.me/r/amazon/B085J3DF8S?fc=us&ds=1

3. https://alsoby.me/r/amazon/B086R3HVRQ?fc=us&ds=1

4. https://alsoby.me/r/amazon/B086R8HMKK?fc=us&ds=1

5. https://alsoby.me/r/amazon/B085X2Q4LV?fc=us&ds=1

6. https://alsoby.me/r/amazon/B085X3L55M?fc=us&ds=1

7. https://alsoby.me/r/amazon/B085X2R3XL?fc=us&ds=1

8. https://alsoby.me/r/amazon/B07HGCRRSX?fc=us&ds=1

9. https://alsoby.me/r/amazon/B07J2VN5RY?fc=us&ds=1

10. https://alsoby.me/r/amazon/B07JN828F8?fc=us&ds=1

11. https://alsoby.me/r/amazon/B07N6MYF6Z?fc=us&ds=1

Comics and Coffee Case Files starring Kirby Jackson and Gambit

Book 1: Marvels, Mochas, and Murder[12]
Book 2: Lattes and Lies[13]
Book 3: Cold Brew Catastrophe[14]
Book 4: Decaf Deceit[15]

---

12. https://alsoby.me/r/amazon/B07J2TFBCB?fc=us&ds=1

13. https://alsoby.me/r/amazon/B07MRCJ56R?fc=us&ds=1

14. https://alsoby.me/r/amazon/B07NKTHCDG?fc=us&ds=1

15. https://alsoby.me/r/amazon/B07SYC5MV5?fc=us&ds=1

About Christine Zane Thomas

Christine Zane Thomas is the pen name of a husband and wife team. A shared love of mystery and sleuths spurred the creation of their own mysterious writer alter-ego.

While not writing, they can be found in northwest Florida with their two children, their dachshund Queenie, and schnauzer Tinker Bell. When not at home, their love of food takes them all around the South. Sometimes they sprinkle in a trip to Disney World. Food and Wine is their favorite season.

About Paula Lester

Sign up for Paula's newsletter to receive information on book releases, other fun information, book recommendations, promos, and more: https://sendfox.com/lp/10q2rm
You can see all of Paula's books at: www.paulalester.com

***

Works by Paula Lester:

***

**Beachside Books Magical Cozy Mysteries
(Co-Authored with Lisa B. Thomas)**
Pasta, Pirates and Poison
Apples, Actors and Axes
Grits, Gamblers and Grudges
Candy, Carpenters and Candlesticks
Meatballs, Mistletoe and Murder
Honey, Hearts and Homicide

***

**Crystal Springs Cozy Witch Mysteries
(Co-Authored with M.E. Harmon)**
Dead Witch Talking (prequel novella)
A Witch Too Late
A Witch Too Hot
A Witch Too Bright
A Witch Too Dead

A Witch Too Frozen
A Witch Too Soon

***

Isles of Mer Cozy Witch Mysteries
(Co-Authored with M.E. Harmon)
Sandy Seances
Seaside Spells
Bewitched Breakers

***

Cruise Ship Cozy Mysteries
(Co-Authored with M.E. Harmon)
Cruising for a Bruising
Angling for a Strangling
Yearning for a Burning

***

Sunnyside Retired Witches Community Mysteries
Ghostly Trails
A Bottle Full of Djinn
Loony Town
Mummy Issues
Clairvoyant Clues
Boss Blues
Engine Repairs
Wedding Whack
Turnabout Time

***

Sunnyside Magical Bakery Cozy Mysteries
Sugar Skulls and Suspects
Tea Tarts and Trespassers
Mint Macarons and Murderers

***

Superior Bay Witch Doctor Mysteries
Witch Doggone Killer?
The Affairs of Witches
Witch Way Out?

***

Unfamiliar Magic Mysteries
Infurior Magic

***

Tessa Randolph Grim Reaper Cozy Mysteries
(Co-Authored with Christine Zane Thomas)
Grim and Bear It
The Scythe's Secrets
Reap What She Sows

www.ingramcontent.com/pod-product-compliance
Lightning Source LLC
Chambersburg PA
CBHW021401150726
47989CB00005B/2348